The Secret Child
(l'Enfant secret)

The Secret Child
(l'Enfant secret)

by

Jean-Michel Olivier

Translated from the French by
Laurence Moscato

Skomlin
House of Memory

Skomlin
House of Memory and Imagination
For more information visit *www.skomlin.com*

A Skomlin Book
Melbourne, Australia

First published with the title *L'Enfant Secret* in Switzerland in 2003
Published by arrangement with Jean-Michel Olivier.
English translation by Laurence Moscato © 2018
Introduction © Clorinda Donato

The moral right of Jean-Michel Olivier to be identified as author has been asserted. Laurence Moscato asserts her right to be identified as translator of the work.

ISBN: 978-0-6482521-5-3 *(paperback)*
ISBN: 978-0-6482521-6-0 *(eBook)*

A catalogue record for this book is available from the National Library of Australia

The paper used in this publication meets the minimum requirements of ANSI/NISO Z39.48-1992 (R1997) (Permanence of Paper). The paper used in this book is from responsibly managed forests. Printed in the United States of America, the United Kingdom and Australia by Lightning Source, Inc.

This publication is a project of the *Clorinda Donato Center for Global Romance Languages and Translation Studies* at California State University, Long Beach, California, United States.

Dedicated to the memory of our late colleague, Dr. Claudia Gosselin, whose commitment to the art of translation was exceeded only by her devotion to students

Finding the Secret Child
A Journey in Translation, Transformation, and Reimagining

Jean-Michel Olivier's 2010 novel, *L'Enfant secret*, is a profoundly personal exploration of those secrets we all inherit almost as part of our DNA. It is a foray into the hidden deeds and misdeeds of our ancestors about which we often know little but that we can sometimes discover through the inadvertent confession of a distant cousin or a box of photos suddenly unearthed. These rare moments of clarity are what Olivier pieces together into a whole—his whole, their whole, and finally ours as well.

Through alternating moments of insight and blindness in the narration, Olivier tells the story of his two sets of grandparents: first Julien and Emilie in the country villages of the French-speaking canton of Vaud in Switzerland, then Antonio and Nora, in the cosmopolitan Trieste, Italy. As Olivier has stated, the history of these people entails a confluence of their different shores, currents, and desires, but while pushing the personal narrative forward he makes it resonate far beyond the chance meeting by his parents that forever merged the destinies of two sides, one Vaudois, the other Italian.

As if by pantomime, Olivier deftly pieces together his parents' and grandparents' lives and his eternal presence within them, while at the same time placing them on the stage of history personified by Benito Mussolini, the principal object of his Italian grandfather's camera and source of livelihood during "Il Duce's" reign. Viewed through this private lens, the Duce's public persona is resized to match a single, unencumbered gaze. Paradoxically, the narrator's ability to see what is in the photos comes through his visually impaired grandfather whose diminished eyesight prompts him to see behind and beyond.

As we follow the narrator seeking himself in the fragments of his grandparents' past and weaving them into his own story, we begin imagining our own histories through his implicit invitation to do likewise. The novel-memoir's impressionistic prose alternates with lacunae that evoke comparable spaces in our memories that spring from both a personal and a universal consciousness. These openings invite us to contemplate what has come earlier and provide mental and emotional connections with what will come later. Filling in those blank spaces with our own narration, the narrator's history thus becomes more solidly ours—a story we have told to ourselves and that we will tell the world.

Olivier's deft amalgamation of personal and public memory enables us to see ourselves embedded in the past—both public and private—and provides insight into the foibles of those who loom large on the pages of history such as Mussolini. This personal narrative thus inspires us to become responsible actors on the stage of history by providing valuable perspectives and incentives for doing so.

Seamlessly merging micro-and-macro-histories, Olivier demonstrates our responsibilities as human beings to be present to the past in order to be present to the future. We eventually discover that Olivier is *l'enfant secret* who inherits and synthesizes the traits of his blind and intuitive grandfather, Julien, and his documentarian grandfather, Antonio, thereby enabling him to record his own truth and become present to his future and to the public memory that we, all of us, ultimately compose.

The book you are reading in English owes extraordinary credit to translator Laurence Moscato. With exacting attention to its several linguistic registers, regional differences and the author's own relationship to the language of his craft, including Italian, Moscato's expert translation conveys not just the literal meaning of the words of the original but more particularly their essence. Indeed, the literature of *Romandie*—French-speaking Switzerland—reminds us how important it is to remember the specificity of Swiss French-speaking identity and the long history of language and literature that both connects it with, but also very much separates it from France.

Jean-Michel Olivier himself has commented on the exile status of any Swiss author who writes in French, required to transform the language of the Other and make it his own, as did Jean-Jacques Rousseau, Charles Ferdinand Ramuz and countless more throughout time. These differences are evident in a number of passages, but especially in the dialogue among the family members at celebratory gatherings and, of course, in culinary descriptions. When translating Olivier's Swiss French, Moscato was keenly aware of the *écart*—the distance separating France from Switzerland and the uneasy relationship that Swiss French writers have with a French language that they must constantly provoke and test in order to render it capable of speaking their truth. It is this distance that makes the text Swiss.

In her translation, Laurence Moscato sought to maintain that distance so as to allow the text's "unfamiliarity" to define its Swiss character. She has described the work of translating *L'Enfant secret* as one in which word and image needed to meld seamlessly: "They are not simply words on a page but images, and not just images or snapshots of intersecting lives but a kind of poem set to a particular music that needed to be transposed in order to communicate the resonance of Jean-Michel Olivier's voice as *l'Enfant secret* became *The Secret Child.*" Thus author and translator have collaborated in producing what might be termed a linguistic symbiosis.

Reading this expert translation of a significant literary work will remind you that much of our own destiny derives from the attributes and actions of our forbearers who, in performing their past, inevitably also perform our future. Delving deeply enough to discover the connection is the challenge that confronts us.

Clorinda Donato
California State University
Long Beach,California

I

It is the turn of the century, in a farmyard; the image is still blurry.

A child is playing with a ball. His name is Julien. He is eight, or nine perhaps. He is running around among rabbits, geese, and hens, while his father, sleeves rolled up, is chopping wood.

It is a warm day; it is autumn.

The man wipes his forehead, then takes up his work again, tirelessly, as the child frolics around him.

Suddenly, the ball bounces off the block and the boy rushes forth to catch it.

He doesn't see his father splitting wood. He doesn't see the axe falling like a flash of lightning. He doesn't see the sky abruptly opening up.

The man didn't see anything either.

Or rather, he saw the child appear out of nowhere, but too late, the axe was already crashing downward.

It struck the child on the back of the head and blood spurted.

Straight away the father started in with the child. But when he saw he was crying and the blood flowing from his head, he calmed down, this justice of the peace of the Côte Vaudoise.

To the mother who was screaming, he said it was only a scratch, and that the child should have known better than to play underfoot. That it would serve him right.

The mother cleaned up the blood: It was spattered all over the place, on his face, on his hands, on his clothes.

When she had finished, the child stopped crying, miraculously, as if he were cured.

Then the mother told herself that the man was right. He was always right.

They wrapped the child's head in a towel, very tightly, to stop the hemorrhage.

This is the first image in my story: a sacrifice in the countryside.

In the days that follow, there is so much work.

The wood needs to be brought in, the hay turned over in the fields, and the grapes still waiting in the vineyards.

The child complains of headaches, of dizzy spells. His legs don't seem to work. He tells his mother about the snow invading his eyes: a strange kind of snow, red and sticky, floating around his head. And his mother consoles him as best she can, she makes him herbal tea, chamomile with honey.

It is a time of violence and secrets.

If anything happens in a family (a meeting, an accident, an emotion), it is forbidden to talk about it. It is cast into oblivion. It is erased from every memory.

Then, the order that reigns supreme is the law of silence.

The first image we have of Emilie is a young girl with a limp; she is surrounded by her brothers and sisters.

There are many of them, five, six, seven, I can't remember. In those days people had large families.

Emilie is the eldest. She looks severe as if aged beyond her years. She is dressed in a summer frock, green ribbons in her hair. She is wearing shoes with buckles, in fashion at the time, but her right foot is slightly bent, a discrete gesture that nonetheless shows up in every photo, like a signature, for one of her legs is shorter than the other and she tries to hide it.

Like Julien, she lives in the country, in the neighboring village. They have never met. Her only pleasure, for now, is the Saturday night dance. She never misses a single one, even if it means walking for hours on dirt roads, buffeted by the wind, the rain, or even snow, so much does she love to dance.

This is the second image in my story: a woman, at nightfall, limping towards the lights of a village fair.

Music is Anton's passion as well and also his reason for living.

At this time in my story, he is a child, like Julien and Emilie, but he, unlike them, lives in Trieste, a city that belongs to Austria. He has been given a name that he is about to abandon, or rather translate (betray) into a foreign language, and takes care of his two younger sisters whom he guards jealously.

Here is the third image. It is not quite clear yet, not yet fully developed: a child whose destiny is travel, insouciance, light, and dispossession.

It is around this time that we find Nora, though farther South, in that area of the Austro- Hungarian Empire that today is called Slovenia.

She is ten, a redhead, pink ribbons in her braids. She is in a blue uniform, the one Fiume orphans wear, and she is always quiet, as if effaced.

No one looks at her. It is as if she weren't there.

But I can see her: she is sitting in the large cafeteria hall, among the other boarders; the sisters are doling out the soup. It's her, I'm sure of it, at the beginning of her story, a story that is also my own, in this noisy hall that smells of cabbage, potatoes, and boiled lard.

I take another look: she is not unhappy in the midst of class-mates her own age, she eats properly, she smiles, and always speaks in even tones.

The fourth image does not exist; it is a totally white photograph, as if the shutter had remained stuck.

A disappearance.

Julien was born in a small village of the Côte Vaudoise, in the farm that today is still called *la triste maison* (the sad house) because the bedrooms face North, looking out at the Jura mountains, while the stable and the outbuildings face South.

Eysins is where he spent his childhood together with his brothers and sisters, in the house of the illustrious ancestors, Juste and Urbain, the very house that welcomed Sainte-Beuve in 1838 for a week's vacation in Switzerland.

A puny baby from the moment he is born, he cries continuously.
"Just bleed him at the neck! yell the neighbors. Take him away, far away!"
Julien survives these curses and the neighbors quiet down.

Emilie was born in the neighboring village, in Borex, on the road connecting Nyon and Divonne. She is the eldest of seven children.

It is still a period when children eat in the kitchen with the servants.

The patriarch eats alone at his table, while his wife, seated on a chair, holds her plate on her lap, eyes lowered to the ground.

Always the first one up in the morning, the one who works the hardest, the last one to complain, Emilie.

She often misses school so she can take care of her brothers and sisters. It is no big deal since these are not times when you go to school in the hopes of one day continuing your education. At least not in her family.

If you do go to school it is in order to learn to read and write—but most of all to learn how to count

The children seem to look upon school as something akin to Purgatory, a waiting place, before they enter into adulthood; then, it is time to start getting serious: girls are taught housekeeping and boys become part of the workforce.

On those days when the weather makes the outside world irresistible, he pines away, yearning to be on the other side of the closed classroom windows; deaf to the instructor's voice, he takes flight with the birds longing to enjoy the warm sun on the rocks, the clouds in the sky.

Because of his poor eyesight, neither a clockmaker, nor a cobbler, nor a baker, nor a high-precision worker will he be. But in no way is his personality affected by this: what Julien likes most is to joke and have a good time, to sing in the village chorus, to play ninepins, to set off in search of birds-nests, to go fishing in the stream, and to disappear on solitary ramblings on country roads.

And also his thick glasses make him look like a poet: this is something girls find quite attractive.

There are days when he is able to see the world with staggering clarity, his is a world in miniature, where the people are but half-pints: busy, silent and sly Lilliputians, buried under artificial snowflakes. On other days, absolute quiet, a never-ending black and mauve dusk, not a star in the heavens, and not a living soul on earth.

Once a year, the school-master assembles the students in the courtyard and gathers them around the monument dedicated to the illustrious ancestors for the traditional class photograph.

This year the Eysins children are included, and the ones from Borex as well. The master is on the right, hands clasped behind his back, a felt hat perched on his head, and a worried look on his face. The Borex school-mistress is standing near the monument. She is wearing a dress with a small collar and a bright-colored smock.

If we look closely, we can make out Julien on the right: he is seated, arms folded across his chest and looking elsewhere, off into the distance. Right beneath him, seated on the monument steps, is Emilie. She is wearing a checkered dress with a Peter Pan collar.

I like to believe that they met for the first time on that particular day in front of the photographer's lens. They know nothing of each other. They are not acquainted. But the photographer, by freezing their image as if in a postcard, has already linked their destinies

It is the luck of the draw: this story that has exploded between the sea and the mountains, and here I am, almost a century later, attempting to piece together a few of its fragments to make sense of it all. It is not the story of my life, but the wanderings and the encounters, the disappointments, the hopes and dreams of which I am, though reluctant to admit it, the secret child.

You won't find many smiles in the photographs of that time; instead, tight-lipped, stony- faced expressions, sleepwalker or even gangster mugs, blank stares.

You would have to wonder if anyone had anything like real fun during this period.

Most probably laughter did exist off-camera and it was photography itself that was a somewhat intimidating ritual, especially in the eyes of those whose images had never been frozen in time. All it took was a photographer to set up a tripod for his camera in the courtyard of a school or in the main square of a village for everyone to assume an "appropriate" pose — in other words a serious and impenetrable expression: a blank mask.

Was it perhaps that these nameless men and women were frightened by the artist in a surgeon's white gown who demanded absolute silence all the time? Or were they perhaps waiting for the little bird who was taking forever to come out of the camera?

I think that they were fearful that someone or something would steal their soul: in everyone's eyes, photography is a magical ceremony where absolutely no one — the children like the grandfather, the baker like the village mayor, the midwife like the bone setter—not a single one of them can rest assured that he or she will emerge unscathed.

Thus, those closed-up visages, determined neither to speak, nor to betray any of their secrets. They seem to be continually murmuring: *Never shall I allow you to come in.*

Julien's patronymic has been established in Switzerland since 1250: in other words, it is deeply rooted in the thick black earth of the Coast.

For nearly seven centuries, he has been from here: he owns a piece of land and a name (recognized by other people). He is not torn between languages. He has never even thought about leaving his land.

There are very few images here on the Coast. Jean Calvin has come through and left his mark. Any images that were left, he threw them into the great fire of the Reformation.

No images — but a fertile and painful imagination.

In his slow-moving dusk, Julien still dreams in color: he can make out shadows, shapes with no clear outline, red, green, blue spots of light, scarlet rain, trees with mauve colored leaves.

For him, the world is a photograph that he will never be able to develop.

What are Emilie's dreams?

In her village, dreaming is frowned upon, especially now, right in the middle of a World War; you want to hold on to something solid: like a proper trade, a serious husband, a stable employment.

Emilie does have dreams of course, but she dreams in secret.

Every night, she dreams of the city, city gentlemen, city pleasures, city money and the liberty which that money will bring to her: it is her life, but in reverse. She has made plans to leave, but she is waiting for the right moment to disappear.

The secret child does not dream: he bears within him all the dreams that are not his, the ambitions, the ineffable desires of others.

Inside his memory, nothing gets discarded, but everything is kept in a jumble, like a junk-dealer's shop: yellowed images (some blurry, others unbearably focused), forgotten tunes, the bright glare of the lake in autumn, the chestnut trees in bloom, blows from an axe, and bursts of laughter.

Julien has left school; he has no diploma; he is all thumbs and cannot shake the reputation of one who never gives a hand. He is hired as a worker in the fields. He helps with the hay, he pulls beets out of the earth, he pulls up weeds, he earths up potatoes. He hunts down potato beetles.

One day the village mayor comes to fetch him: strong men are needed to build a road over there in the mountain, between Saint-Cergue and Nyon.

Julien signs up right away. Tirelessly, he digs into the earth with a pickaxe, extracts roots and stones, pours and spreads boiling tar that will burst in winter under the assault of freezing temperatures and in summer will have to be sprinkled with pebbles during heat waves.

One evening they met for the first time; they laughed; they drank white wine (Chasselas that tends to scratch the back of the throat), they danced until their heads started spinning and being together was so wonderful that now they are never apart.

Seen from afar, they make a strange couple, those two: the man with the thick lenses perched on his nose, twirling his dance partner without quite knowing where he is headed, and the woman following him, looking, solemn and resolute, her right leg dragging behind her.

This is my image of them, accordion and clarinet in the background. And here is their dialogue:

She: has he noticed? Will he still marry me?

He: has she noticed that I am blind as a bat? Will she still marry me?

Last night, I dreamt that he could see.

Or rather that Julien could see me, the one who is writing about him and whom he has never seen.

Even if it didn't really happen that way, I like to think that the last woman he would be able to see is also the first one. Emilie, the one he will marry: a single image on his retina.

After that he will draw the curtain.

Julien likes shade and gentian liqueur, Lyonnaise ninepins, pork delicatessen meats and cool wine from the Coast, he likes rubbing his lenses clean after he has covered them with mist, solitary ramblings in the vineyards, playing cards with his brothers, crooning songs he learned in the men's choir (*Amitié et Gaîeté*), rye bread and cheese, vegetable broth, and reading large print news-paper headlines.

In the photos, you can see a group of men, most of them quite young, bare torsos glistening with sweat, pickaxe in hand, lost in the middle of nature, and, amongst them, there is one who is looking elsewhere, off into the distance: it is Julien.

He is wearing a cap and looks quite jovial, as usual.

The road cuts through the forest. You can see the trees on either side: in front, the ones that must be chopped down, and, behind them, the ones that must be uprooted, a long and arduous task, for they have been rooted deeply in the grey Jura earth since the beginning of time.

Nature, the great outdoors, the sparkling sun: these are the elements that Julien, like Emilie, cherishes.

They find it unbearable to be cooped up inside for more than ten minutes, otherwise they suffocate, they wither away like flowers in need of water, they become depressed.

They both possess the same love for the earth, for the mountains that protect the horizon, for the lake that creates a hole of light as you face south: this is where they belong, where they are rooted, a place like no other—even if they do not own a single acre of land.

Emilie likes order and silence, riding the little red train that goes all the way to Barillette, playing the local lottery, claret wine and head-cheese, making *brice-lets* (Vaudois waffles), getting a pedicure once a month, collecting 50 centime coins that she keeps in cigar tubes, reading the newspapers *Le Journal de Nyon* and *L'Echo Illustré*, drinking a drop of Port on Sundays after church, taking care of her brothers and sisters, cooking for a large group of people and dancing the waltz.

Emilie and Julien were married in the Eysins church on May 6, 1922.

Back then, a wedding was something that belonged to everyone. A horse-drawn carriage with a bench transported the betrothed to the church: she in a lace dress and a short white veil, he in a brown three-piece-suit, a white carnation in his buttonhole, glasses perched on his nose; and the pastor celebrated the union amidst screaming children.

After the church ceremony, a wedding reception. And what a reception!

White wine flowed, tears were shed, kisses were exchanged under the great chestnut trees, toasts were offered to the young newly-weds, more tears were shed, and dancing continued throughout the night.

They even had a photographer come all the way from Lausanne just to immortalize the occasion.

Two days after the wedding, Julien is back at work.

We see him on the mountain, surrounded by his mates, clearing out the underbrush.

In this image, even if he is looking elsewhere, off into the distance, he cuts a fine figure, with his glistening torso, his muscular arms, his jaunty cap. He enjoys this man-to-man struggle with the trees, the roots, and the stones under the hot sun.

At noon, they all break out their lunch-boxes. They go sit on tree trunks in the shade and everything is shared: soup, bread and cheese, while a bottle of white wine is passed from hand to hand.

Frequently the road between the mountain and the village grows long. There are many cafés along the way. And Julien is late coming home.

Everyone knows him. They wave to him from afar. They offer to buy him a drink. Wine glasses line up on the table. Stories of cuckold husbands and wives get told. A good time is had by all. Fatigue seems to have totally vanished.

When night falls, Julien inevitably cries out as he looks at his watch: *"Merde!* I'm in for it yet again!"

Emilie and Julien navigate between two languages: proper French that is spoken in cities with a pointed accent, and Vaudois dialect, which is the everyday language.

When they go into town, they make an effort to speak like everyone else, without mistakes, and sometimes it isn't easy because people from Lausanne or Genève chatter at such a pace and you can't understand everything they say, they use barbaric words, like those in books, expressions that you have never heard around here.

They are a little bit lost, like foreigners. But they get their revenge later when a fellow from the city comes to visit them. They have fun peppering the discussion with country words and idioms. At every turn, they bring up this *roille* endlessly falling and *grande fricasse* and *cupesse* and the poor man is utterly lost. He bombards them with questions. He feels he has landed in the midst of some unknown savage tribe.

The secret child does not grow: he has always lived among shadows and silence, but he doesn't miss a thing. And he listens behind doors, the child with the detective eyes, behind walls, and behind the bodies around him, he records the sounds belonging to the realm of the world, the living and the dead—but as if from the inside.

He remains as he is. Never will his voice change. Never will his body become an adult's body.

Heart of the *infans:* outside the realm of words, light, or revelation.

A birth secret.

Julien's parents have died. The family domain (the farm, the orchards, the fields) has been dismembered. Like his brothers and sisters, Julien has received his portion of the inheritance. He has chosen to reoccupy the Duillier Pub.

It is in a magnificent location: a long and narrow two-story construction situated right at the entrance to the village, a stone's throw from the Château that was built in the 12th century by Etienne de Crassie, and, once managed by his ancestor, Urbain. A large, cinder block esplanade with a chestnut-tree and a plane tree occupies the front of the inn that dominates the vineyards and enjoys an exceptional view of the lake and the Alps.

This is where Julien and Emilie set up house on a beautiful morning in February of 1926.

Emilie is pregnant. How she cursed the heavens when she found out! She tried old wives' remedies, abortive herbal brews.

But, nothing doing: despite everything, a child is growing in her womb; it will be born in August, right at the hottest time of the year; it will be a boy, she just knows it, a big fat baby that will be forever hanging on to her breast, and she already hates him.

Tonight at Duillier, what a celebration! The entire village has gathered for the house-warming and re-opening of the renovated pub with its freshly stuccoed walls. A resurrection...

The weather is perfect. It is the beginning of summer.

Julien has hung lanterns on the branches of the chestnut tree. The tables are covered with large white tablecloths, mountains of French fries, dishes with delicatessen meats and cheese, white wine for everyone.

With her enormous stomach, Emilie has trouble walking, but, still, she is enjoying herself.

He is a secret child, without a face and without a voice.

He has always been there, but he has not yet seen the light.

As if he were at the theatre, he remains in the shadows, never speaks a word, but is ready to leap out on the stage.

In the garden below, Julien has planted two varieties of cabbage, yellow carrots, peas, string beans, lettuce, turnips, cardoons, asparagus, strawberries and blackberry bushes. Julien spends hours there, sowing, weeding, hoeing, breaking apart rebellious chunks of earth, setting up the garden patches, trimming trees and bushes, watering each plant with an artist's delicate touch...

Downstairs is where Emilie reigns supreme: her territory is the kitchen where bunches of onions and braids of garlic and of corn, sausages and salt pork hang from the smoke-blackened ceilings.

People flock to the inn from as far away as Gimel and Nyon, from Saint-Livres, from Divonne, from Geneva just to taste Emilie's specialties: *"la fricassée de lièvre ou de lapin"*, hare or rabbit fricassee, *"la langue de boeuf aux câpres"* beef tongue with capers, *"la tête de porc marbrée,"* headcheese *"la tarte au raisiné,"* compote tart — and of course the famous *malakoffs!*

These are cheese fritters made from a recipe that she inherited from an old mercenary from the Coast who had once been in the Crimean war and had contributed to the fall, in1855, of the Malakoff Fort that protected Sebastopol.

Here is her recipe: she cuts up the cheese (one that is on the salty side) in small sticks about as thick as a thumb, then marinates them in white wine. Meanwhile, she prepares the batter, mixing flour, eggs and milk, with a pinch of salt. She removes the cheese from the wine and rolls the sticks in flour before dipping them in the batter, then deep-fries them in sesame oil (boiling at 180 degrees C) until they turn a beautiful golden color. Finally she wipes the malakoffs on a kitchen towel that absorbs the extra oil and serves them on a dish together with an appetizing green salad.

August 1926: birth of Petit Pierre.

In honor of this happy event, Julien has invited the entire village to a celebration on the terrace of the Pub.

This summer is superb. There is singing under the tall chestnut tree. The lake could be a painting by Hodler. The air is so pure, you can see the entire French coast all the way from the Point of Yvoire to the Geneva Water Geyser!

Morning or night, the pub is always full. In just a few months it has become the bar of choice. Emilie's cooking has conquered the food-lovers who come back for more in ever- increasing numbers. Julien, who is in charge of the reception and the wine, has attracted all the party-lovers as well as all the worshippers of Bacchus. He has set up, in a corner of the immense terrace, a game of nine-pins for the children. He has also built with his own hands a large clear-water shallow pond in which trout and gray carp can be seen swimming.

In her kitchen, Emilie is beside herself: she doesn't know which way to turn — and the little one crying in his cradle...

This is my own story, this story I am writing: the secret child who is bleeding within me and who has come from such a distance, Austria and Italy, Slovenia and Switzerland, Eastern Europe.

He has crossed so many borders and spoken so many languages!

The very first law, inculcated from early childhood, is that you must obey. It is not the law of the jungle, but the swift justice of families. To this end, in Emilie and Julien's room, right above the mirror, hangs the leather whip.

Pierre can see it whenever he passes by and he knows that it will be used unsparingly should he not toe the line.

Could this be why, so often, the child stands frozen at the threshold?

Pierre: the little one who gets stuffed with food and still cries for more; the louder he bawls, the more they stuff his mouth with fruit, corn puree, milk and chestnuts. He devours everything he is wanting, anything that comes within reach of his mouth.

We can see him in a photo taken when he was three, full chubby cheeks, short hair, with very big, very dark eyes that seem to eat up his face, mouth distorted in a cry.

Julien's latest craze: a small second-hand camera bought from the hawker who comes through every year to sell pots and knives, linen for the house, subscriptions to *L'Almanach du Messager boiteux*.

As they share a jug of white wine, the man shows him how to open the camera body and carefully insert the Kodak film, then close the camera back up, away from the light to keep the film from being burnt, how to calculate and set the shooting distance and finally press down with a finger to release the shutter.

And the rest is magic.

From that moment on, Julien shoots at anything that moves, at everything he loves, at everything he is going to lose.

He cannot see very clearly what it is he is photographing. He can distinguish outlines, but they are blurred. He can discern colors, but they are in constant motion. He does recognize faces, but he can never see their expression. He lets a voice, a scent, a familiar gesture be his guide.

He, who in photographs is always looking elsewhere, is on the prowl to capture his immediate surroundings.

Camera slung around his neck, thick lenses perched on his nose, Julien stores up images.

When they are developed, he is always astonished at what he sees. It never is quite what he thought he had photographed. The poses are different, the faces uncertain, at times the characters jut out of the frame. You can make out only an arm or a leg, a shoulder, only part of the face.

Impossible to tell who they belong to.

He is not discouraged by this; quite the contrary, he snaps away with renewed energy.

Julien is convinced that one day — a day in the far-off future no doubt — he will see these images with different eyes. Meanwhile, he is creating memories for himself: an enchanted kingdom that he is constantly enriching and that he will cherish in his old age.

As far back as he can remember, snow has been falling in his eyes, a pale and heavy snow; at times it is tinged with bright red, at times it falls in blue irregular snowflakes. It is a flurry of flakes, or it is an avalanche in slow motion; and every time, he is in the front row, powerless, dazed, alone in the eye of the storm.

Julien closes his eyes: immediately, beached on the sand, appears a child's shoe glistening in the blue marine light. Julien opens his eyes, then shuts them again. The small sandal is still there, central and white, embedded like a shell on the back of the eye.

Julien repeats the process a hundred times, and a hundred times the little sandal beckons, upside-down, mysterious, fluorescent.

He closes one eye, then the other. No sandal. Nothing but a skylight opening onto obscure reality, blinding self-evidence, drowning under the onslaughts of crimson snow. The sandal appears only when both eyelids are sealed. When he opens only one eye, Julien sees nothing.

"A sandal that only appears every other time! It's enough to drive you mad, Doctor…"

" Absolutely not, my dear Sir! Hallucinations occur frequently, especially in a case like yours…"

"A case like mine?"

"Yes, long-standing, complex and, in a word, desperate."

"Is it that serious, Doctor?"

"We will run some tests, naturally, just to be sure… But they will be inconclusive, as always. Is it macular degeneration? A simple dislocation of the retina? (although a dislocation, especially if it is in the wrong place, never turns out to be simple). Could it even be something else? As of now, I am not in a position to tell you anything."

"But, you see, Doctor, a white sandal beached on a sandbar, that cannot be commonplace!"

"I grant you that, Sir."

"Well then, why a sandal?"

"As for that, I am unable to answer you. It is not within the realm of my expertise. You might want to consult a psychoanalyst."

"A what?"

"Someone who handles this kind of nonsense. There are specialists…"

"Doctors who specialize in sandals?"

"In a way, my dear Sir. A psychoanalyst is the only one who might enlighten you as to the meaning of your phantasms. My own field of expertise, is the eye: its structure, its nature, and its diseases. What you see — or, in your case, think you see — is none of my business."

The test results were inconclusive. Or rather not quite: they detected a growing edema in both eyes, probably the consequence of a thrombosis of the central retinal vein.

"Is it serious, Doctor?" asks Julien who has not grasped a single word of the explanation offered him by the specialist in the white gown.

"The case is certainly not simple. But often the most complex cases are the most interesting."

"Does that mean surgery?"

"Surgery would be useless."

"Why, Doctor?"

"We shall let nature run its course. It is normal for the edema to get worse before it starts to be resorbed (if one day it is resorbed, though I don't believe that will happen). It could take six months or even up to ten years before it becomes stable. It can get worse, remain stationary or even get better. However, you are lucky, my dear Sir!"

"Why, Doctor?"

"Because you don't suffer from distorting waves, nor do you have a dark curtain in your eye."

"And this is lucky, Doctor?"

"Yes, even very lucky! For the sandal that you see (or think you see, let's not quibble), you are able to see it quite clearly, as if it really existed…"

"But, for goodness' sake, it does really exist, this sandal! For I see it as I see you, Doctor!"

"No matter! Your hallucinations have the strength of reality, my dear Sir. That is your good fortune."

Pierre is three. He bumbles around the kitchen like a bee: he tastes every dish, he dips his lips in the wine glasses, he knocks over stacks of plates, he hides under the tables.

His mother does all she can to keep him away, but to no avail: the kid is forever underfoot! They have just bought an old phonograph and the child enjoys watching it spin, with the big black shiny record, the slightly squeaky needle, and the music coming out of the metal horn.

The customers enjoy it too: the old tangos, the Maurice Chevalier songs, and the old Fréhel standbys. So they come in droves, especially on Saturdays and Sundays, when they can lunch on the terrace facing the mountains that sparkle in the sun.

Sometimes, in Autumn, he sets off without a by your leave, carrying his cane and his small Rollei. He follows the white mountain road, that well-loved road, that smells of harvest, oxen-drawn carts, wet leaves. Patches of mist rising from the fields.

He reaches Arzier, walks through the village and heads up to the stone quarries where he stops in the middle of the pine trees and fossils to eat his picnic lunch. Then, it is time for him to head down towards Bassins, the Burgundian cemetery, the immense rye and corn fields, and finally on to the Café de la Cézille where he quenches his thirst with a jug of white wine to accompany the owner's delicious home-made deli style pork meats.

The return trip to Begnins is difficult. The descent is steep, the vineyards shimmer in the setting sun, his legs are going numb. He makes it to the village, collapses in a chair in a corner of the inn, exhausted but radiant, orders five glasses of Chasselas wine, and falls asleep on the table.

Many are the roads Julien has taken!

He can't remember a time when, upon closing his eyes, he didn't see himself once again walking along these rocky paths. Always a solitary figure in pursuit of a shadow, the cry of a bird, the mauve-colored stain of a pond.

Once in a while, he takes a photograph. More often than not, as if hypnotized, he advances blindly, guided only by that smell of ground fruit, of dead leaves, of freshly cut hay. The deeper he advances, the more he feels the ground slipping away from under him. No longer of this world, he is again as he was before: river, fern, long shadow on the ground.

Paradise has no image.

He walks on the edge of the abyss, towards that other part of himself, from a time before the world began, a place we are no longer allowed to enter once our eyes have been opened.

One day, Petit Pierre played some records on the old phonograph. It had rained. The needle grated on the records. Maurice Chevalier had a frog in his throat.

On his own without waiting for permission, he carried the records out to the terrace, one by one, because they are heavy and, he was afraid of breaking them, and then he placed them on the ledge of the low stone wall surrounding the terrace so they might dry out in the sun.

It is August. Heat rises from the vineyards.

Evening. Disaster strikes: almost all of the records have melted. They are scratched and warped because of the heat — impossible to get a sound out of them!

A fortune evaporated in the sun.

Forever crouched on all fours, rummaging through trash cans like a fox in search of food, close-cropped head, greedy pimply face, hands reaching down inside the garbage bag, visage smudged with coffee and ashes as teeth crunch down on cat or chicken bones in order to suck out their delicious marrow.

III

Spring. Ten years later.

The orphan has left her country, but she hasn't gone very far.

She has settled in Trieste, a city of some importance at the time, a place of transit for Austrian commerce. German and Italian, and a little Slovenian are spoken here. She has rented a small room in town, and she lives alone; she gives private lessons.

In 1918, everything has changed: Trieste is Italian. Little by little, she will lose that Old European veneer that was the mark of her splendor during the Austrian period: she will once again become a city just like all the others — awaiting the assault of the irredentists under the command of the poet D'Annunzio…

German, which has always prevailed, is to become a minority language, and all those who speak it will have to gradually abandon it since, henceforth, everything will happen in the language of the victors, and Trieste, once so proud of her privileges, receives all her orders from Rome.

As for Anton, something is happening, to be sure: something is breaking, since he has become a foreigner in his own country.

Anton likes fencing and the theatre, strolling around the port of Trieste, pretty girls eating ice- cream, Ezra Pound's poetry, nights spent working in the secret of his dark room, military parades, Irish Whisky (to which he has been introduced by his friend James Joyce who always has a flask of it in his overcoat pocket), *minestrina* with alphabet-shaped pasta, horseback riding, going for a swim in the sea, the music of Grieg, Alban Berg operas, speaking German with a foreign woman, Barbera wine and Parma ham, sacred music, wearing his hair combed back and plastered with brilliantine, saying a prayer before each meal, playing tennis on Sundays.

The Great War is something Nora experienced of course, but in a different way even though she remained in Trieste too. Her dream is to teach in German and

Slovenian, but she has embarked on Italian, the dominating language, which she will soon be speaking perfectly though without rolling her r's, which will give her a special charm

Foreigners are constantly at the beginning of their own story: this is why, wherever she might go, Nora can always feel at home

Nora likes clutter and silence, hats with little veils, Italian opera and Viennese waltzes, old photographs, prune *knödel* drowned in sugar and melted butter, making coffee in small pans covered with dents, sprinkling her hands and neck with Eau de Cologne, listening to Slovenian songs on the radio, sharing the *merenda* (afternoon snack) with the privileged students of the school, going incognito to the movies, swimming in the sea, meditating in the San Vitale church, and recalling the time when Trieste was still Austrian.

Anton was there on that sad day of 1918, when a large Italian ship, the *Audace,* flags unfurled and waving in the wind, took possession of the former irredentist port much to the astonishment of the humiliated Austrians and the jubilation of the triumphant, victorious Italians. He was there, on the very pier that will soon bear the name of that ship and become the promenade of choice of the entire city, the Corso leading up to the emptiness of the sea, and he took no photos.

At that hour of waning light, there is a veritable population of shadows, not exactly dead, nor quite alive who arrange to rendez-vous on the pier of the Audace: little gentlemen with canes and Fedoras, widows walking arm in arm, two by two, insurance salesmen in a hurry, beautiful foreign women fascinated by the noises of the port and the majestic pace of the ocean liners cutting through the waves.

Now Trieste has become a literary capital: The poet Ezra Pound is living here, as well as the enigmatic Italo Svevo. Trieste is also where, not so long ago, an Irish couple, whose extravagance easily matched its fame took up residence: James Joyce and his wife (also named Nora).

He teaches at the Berlitz Language School, juggling languages (English, German, Italian, Greek, French,) just as he will later in *Finnegan's Wake*, the first post Babel book. His trademarks are his monocle (like Julien, James Joyce suffers from poor eyesight), his taste for drinking songs and his walking stick.

Together with his wife, Joyce leads a grand life-style and has no qualms about extorting money from his younger brother Stanislaus (who has joined them in Trieste) whenever he runs out of money, or whenever he feels like buying a new piano.

Of course, Anton didn't witness their arrival in Trieste on that 20th of October 1904, but here is how Alessandro Mancini-Bruno, a Triestino friend, describes the two of them: "Tattered and as ragged as a beggar, he was dragging behind him, with total nonchalance, a suitcase that looked like a skinned hyena.

"Things floating in the wind leaked out from every split in the case, but he didn't seem to be concerned with even attempting to stuff them back inside."

"At some remove, almost buried under her wide-brimmed straw hat and inside the man's jacket that hung well below her knees, Nora Joyce seemed to be a heap of crumpled rags. Stiff as a ramrod, she darted her eyes about her without showing the least bit of emotion."

"Italians from Trieste," Joyce will one day write, "love their country, with the provision that they know which one it is."

Nora is the kind of woman who is not carried and supported by the ground she walks on, but rather by books.

When you are alone in a foreign city, books become your confidants, and even your family.

Now Anton is no longer known as Anton, but as Antonio: just two extra letters (*io* = I) that make a world of difference... Thanks to the same magic operation, he translates his family name (Buchacher) into the language of the victors (Campofaggi).

With a single stroke, he crosses out his Austro-Hungarian origins and shows everyone his willingness to be integrated: he has become a new man who will be more Italian than the Italians.

These multiple betrayals, this playing around with letters, these translations from one language to another, must have occurred for a reason: I don't know what it is, and yet I am intrigued. It is the best-kept secret. When he changed his given name, was Antonio hoping to erase with one easy stroke his foreignness?

Was he afraid that the Italian police, upon looking into his origins might discover one day that his mother was Jewish — and therefore a foreigner *par excellence* — particularly at a time when anti-semitism is becoming more widespread with every passing month?

Nora has a Slovenian name: it begins like a waterfall, fresh and transparent, and ends in a long whisper. It will be her name for twenty-four years, and then she will change it to her husband's name.

Upon her death, at the end of summer in 1981, she will regain her maiden name, following a long-standing custom in Italy that establishes that a widow is to recover her original identity.

Which will be a problem since this is not a name that anyone knows (her husband has been dead for five years and her children have never known it). There will have to be an investigation to recover this lost name, this secret name, that is her very own name — the name of the foreigner that will be engraved on her headstone in the immense Turin cemetery.

In Trieste, Anton is a regular at cafés, churches, concert halls. He plays the organ every Sunday at the Protestant church (music is the only religious element in his life). But, most of all, he has developed a passion for photography.

On a Sunday in May at the flea market of Piazza San Giusto, Antonio bought himself a second-hand Leica, and he shoots at everything and anything around him with obstinance, temerity, and impatience, as if he were trying to give a physical substance to his obsessive phantom.

Antonio is a dancer: a thief of souls. He has always flitted back and forth between music and language, poetry and photography, church and chance encounters with beautiful women.

In the late afternoon, Antonio frequents the Fencing Club of Trieste. He is a fine blade. He enjoys the daring and the danger, the displacements and the fancy footwork. Fencing is a demanding sport, but for Antonio, it is, more than anything else, an art — and a game.

At this time, fencers face each other with unprotected faces, no breastplate, and with an unbuttoned blade. It is not rare that during a particularly relentless attack a blade may slip and pierce the chest of the adversary, at the prime or at the octave. A tiny red flower appears at the place where the tip of the blade has pierced the skin. But that is not enough to cause the halt of the duel. That can only happen if one of the two adversaries surrenders. That is the rule. Once the duel is over, they salute each other. They proceed to the bar of the club where they drink a whiskey or a grappa. They smoke cigars. They engage in a new duel. The evening continues till the crack of dawn. Finally, they leave each other and each goes off to face the violent assaults of the bora.

It often happens that a week later, one of the fencers might be missing because he has neglected to take care of the minuscule wound. Surreptitiously, the hemorrhage has invaded the entire rib cage, asphyxiated the lungs, emptied out the heart.

The valiant fencer has left the world stage without even being aware of it.

Nora's dreams are conventional: she wants a husband, children, and a home. What she has always missed: a family.

For Antonio, dreaming is a significant part of life: it consists of music, poetry, and the cult of images. He loves grand classical music, its fugues, its counterpoint, and variations on a theme. However, he finds opera boring: all those oversized matrons tightly laced and bursting out of costumes a size too small, barely making it to the front of the stage as they sing the agony of a Violetta or of an Aïda, leave him totally cold. Aside from Berg, he has no taste for modern music: even a canary couldn't whistle the works of a Stravinsky, or so he claims.

For him, poetry is the secret language of a chosen few. This is why he is passionate about Ezra's *Cantos* and T.S. Elliot's entire *oeuvre*, the novellas of James Joyce and futurist poems. For Antonio, poetry transcends music and completes it in a certain manner, since it only needs silence (a silent voice) to allow its chords to resound in harmony.

As for images, in Antonio's life they are like a blind spot. It is through them that he will possess the world (even if he is as of yet unaware of it) and that is precisely how, in fact, the world will reveal all of its secrets to him.

At this time, Antonio has not yet acquired a real job: he only has hobbies. He is hardly aware that this is a luxury.

The war has just ended; a certain Benito, who hasn't yet begun to shave his head, is already baring his teeth. Italy is in the throes of reconstruction: the New Order is being established.

Trieste has become an insignificant city, even more distant from Rome than it had been from Vienna. The Austrian splendor has faded away. The commercial port has ceased almost all of its activities in order to become a pleasure port where the great ocean liners on their way to Asia drop anchor.

Trieste is a joyless city, but it is a city where life is good and Antonio likes living there.

And Nora, who does she see in Trieste?

Colleagues from the Berlitz School, where she now teaches, and amongst them, the Joyces. They live near the port in a large apartment, financed in part by Stanislaus, James's brother.

On certain Sundays, they invite Nora to their place on Piazza Ponterosso, below the crosses of the Serbian church where they sometimes attend mass; James installs himself at the piano, monocle tightly wedged in front of his left eye, and croons Irish tunes with his beautiful tenor voice (he has always dreamed of becoming a singer).

"I recognize you, you old bootlegger! We are a border town, a town of smugglers, bandits and not of heroes".

There are other foreigners there, like her, who have come from the four corners of Europe, who do not know English (and certainly not the Dublin dialect), but who pick up the refrain when Jim nods his head at them.

At the Berlitz School, Nora moves in the world of the beautiful people of high society. Her students are often barons and counts, sons of wealthy families, daughters of ambassadors; every one of them treats her with condescension.

Among them is a certain Ettore Schmitz. He manages a paint factory for sardine cans and ship hulls. He is absolutely devoid of self-confidence. He dreams of becoming a great writer. He has already published two novels that have met with no success: *A Life* and *Senilitá* (Senility), the first under the pen name of Ettore Samigli and the second under Italo Svevo — *out of pity for that lone vowel surrounded by six consonants in my name.*

October 28, 1922: Mussolini marches on Rome.

Two days later, in the mail, Antonio receives a dedicated copy of James Joyce's latest novel, *Ulysses*, that he devours in one sitting.

Every morning as soon as he gets up, the first pleasure of the day is to throw the window wide open, close his eyes and fill his lungs with the *bora*, that cool wind that blows in from far out at sea carrying perfumes from the Orient in its trail.

In the afternoon, like every Triestino, he walks along the jetty that connects the city to the Castelnovo castle. The outing is a ritual, a symbol of his belonging to the community. He never forgets to bring his little Leica.

The ritual always includes the savoring of a *cafè corretto* while watching the pretty girls go by.

It is here, on the Audace pier that he encountered Nora for the first time.

It is autumn. She is walking arm in arm with her friends. She is laughing. He invites them to have an ice cream, and then he photographs them on the jetty, which impresses the young women, for this is the first time they have ever seen a camera.

As they are still laughing, Antonio hands them his card.

"The photos will be ready tomorrow. Call me!".

A peal of laughter from the girls. But only Nora, the following day, dialed the number.

Today Nora went to pick up her photos. She remained in the photographer's studio for a long while. They chatted a little, but not much, for Nora is the silent type. She is suspicious of the spoken word, of the secrets that you reveal in spite of yourself; she is a foreigner.

When he showed her the photos, Nora became animated. She laughed when she saw the faces her friends were making as they struck poses like starlets while she, in the center of the image, was squinting because of the sun in her eyes; she thought she looked a bit ridiculous.

Antonio told her he found her scrunched up face charming.

This photograph taken by Antonio on the docks of Trieste, on a Sunday in June, while the mighty *Bora* was blowing and crowds were clustered around the café terraces, this is the first image of their story.

Previously, to be sure, there have been others, secret images, embedded into the wax of memory, but they have not been developed. Unless someone deliberately sets out to retrieve them, they will never come to light.

These phantom images constitute the treasure trove into which I am delving in search of answers, the lost thread of my history, my story.

Trieste with her shady grace, endless alleys in the old city, small piazzas overrun by pigeons, burning bora, blowing in your back, carrying you all the way to the Audace pier: this is where Antonio wanders in the evening, smoking his Virginia cigars, a bottle of grappa in hand, singing barcaroles in honor of the recent memory of Nora's white skin, how he brushed against it in the shadows, that instant of pure joy, miraculous, in front of the image that he has just developed.

This original image (the photo taken in front of the sea) is also what will allow Nora, the woman, the foreigner, to be recognizable in Antonio's gaze.

Through this image, she is embedded in his eyes, in his memory, in his life: would he even have noticed her — or in other words, would he have picked her out from the other women — if he hadn't taken a photo of her on that specific Sunday on a pier swarming with people?

And what about Nora, would she have paid any attention to this totally uninhibited young man with a mustache and white spats, black hair brushed back lustrous with brilliantine, had he not had a camera slung around his neck?

Images of Nora: Antonio has made dozens of them and little by little, without even being aware of it, in the silence of the darkroom, he has developed feelings for this young woman, the foreigner.

They see each other more often. Together, they go to the theater and the movies. They go for walks along the port.

On some evenings, they agree to meet near the Faro della Vittoria, lighthouse (no doubt the only one in the world to be illuminated in pink and blue) and then, without speaking, they walk along the docks. The Verdi Theater shuts its doors. Silence reigns but for the bora and the sound of the sea. Before the lights are turned off (the chairs have already been stacked up on the tables) they go have one last drink of Cognac at the *Caffè degli specchi,* the Café of Mirrors, where Antonio surreptitiously takes out his Leica to steal Nora's visage from her yet again, like a sacred fetish.

With each other, they speak either German or Italian, it depends: Italian is the language of love, and German is for arguing. For they often argue, over little nothings, over trifles, since the young woman also has quite a will of her own

When Nora is alone, she speaks to herself in Slovenian.

Nora is an excellent cook and her specialty, which earns her the envious respect of all her neighbors, is the famous strudel which she makes with brown sugar, according to the old recipes from her country, with almonds and pine-nuts, and a sizable amount of sliced apples; she then brushes the surface with an egg yolk so it will turn golden and sprinkles it with a pinch of cinnamon.

With every passing day, Antonio's feelings for Nora become more definite, and now the image is clear.

The war has been over for six years. Trieste has recovered some of her splendor. Mussolini rules the country with an iron fist. The little king has anointed him as an equal on every level, despite his disgust at the idea of considering this *cafone* (this country bumpkin) this unrefined upstart who has retained the brutal crude ways of the Romagna countryside, who harangues crowds, and who never has qualms about coming to blows and having fistfights in public.

It is time for a wedding.

For this occasion, Nora wears a tiara in her hair and a long gossamer tulle train. Antonio is in a tuxedo, patent-leather shoes, frilled tuxedo shirt, black hair plastered to his head, even his mustache is fully waxed.

The wedding takes place in a small church near Corso Vittorio, the very church where Antonio plays the organ on Sundays, but today, another musician has replaced him at the organ.

It is the church where the exiled Vaudois from the Piemonte come to worship. There is a large crowd. All the Protestants in Trieste are in attendance. Italians, Austrians, Yugoslavs. The vows are pronounced in several languages. The music selections (Bach, Grieg, Pergolesi) have been chosen by Antonio.

After the ceremony, on the church steps, under a light rain that has just begun to fall, the groom himself is the one who photographs the wedding, thanks to the delayed shutter release of his old Leica.

Suddenly the images gather speed: Nora is pregnant. Antonio who splits his time between fencing, his passion for horses, and the nights spent in his dark room, oblivious, has not noticed.

When Nora tells him the news, he is surprised, disconcerted.

"How can that be?

"These things happen, Nora tells him. Especially after what we have done!"

Still stunned by the news, Antonio fetches a bottle of grappa, fills two wine glasses, hands one to Nora, who puts it right down on the table with a grimace of disgust while he downs his own glass in one gulp.

"It will be a boy!" he sings out at the top of his lungs.

It is a girl.

They call her Livia. Antonio is disappointed.

Henceforth, Nora will take care of her little girl. She will learn the gestures of a mother, the mother that she herself never had. She will, in fact, do nothing else: teaching, feeding, changing, swaddling, tending, consoling. Never again will she have another job.

Since someone has to bring home the bacon, Antonio has no choice but to take on all kinds of photography jobs. He will work for newspapers (who pay very poorly). He will cover weddings, banquets and official receptions. He will make billboards, and postcards of Trieste. He will photograph personalities who visit the city, like movie stars, sports idols or even the terrible Storace, the great organizer and director of the New Man, the very same who will prohibit coffee and who will introduce the goose step in military marches.

But, what Campo enjoys more than anything is to take photos of Livia. He puts the naked and intimidated child down on a white blanket in his studio under the eaves, and takes as many shots of her as he can, all the while trying to make her smile. She remains motionless for hours. She never cries. She likes the crude light of the projectors.

Later, when she is older, he will dress her up in preposterous costumes, with fairy veils, ornaments fit for an oriental princess, or his wife's wedding tulle veil and he will enjoy the faces she makes while he photographs her. She will always hold absolutely still for hours on end, bending to her father's every whim with good grace — as good as gold, or, as the saying goes in French, "*sage comme une image*," as well behaved as an image.

For Antonio, reality is not enough: it must always be unmasked or transfigured in order to make it disgorge — for only then does another truth come to light, one that had literally been right in front of everyone's eyes and yet no one had ever, in its blinding evidence, imagined or even glimpsed.

His nights are those of a hunter constantly on the prowl, ears straining, eye at the ready, roving about the alleys he knows by heart from the Audace Pier to the sinister San Giusto cathedral, from the ancient mediaeval city razed by the Austrians to the perfectly designed modern city with its straight grid-like streets; always a flask of grappa in hand and often singing until the first glimmerings of dawn.

Trieste crudely awakening: crude sunlight on the brown tiles of its huddled roofs...

His days are spent lying in wait, insatiable predator, along the wharves swarming with people, in front of the City Hall (*Hôtel de Ville*) or at the train station, wherever cohorts of government officials gather, visiting ministers or simply the ordinary people of Trieste constantly hungry for human contact, laughing loudly and joking about anything and everything.

On an October night in 1929, on his way home, Antonio catches sight of a sports car speeding along the coast. It is a red Alfa Romeo, 3L. The driver is a man with a shaved head in a racer's jumpsuit. At his side, a stunning woman, blond hair held in place with a silk scarf, sunglasses perched on her forehead, lips painted a bright red.

Antonio arms his camera, aims at the red fireball hurtling down the road, and shoots.

Three blinding flashes tear the night asunder. The car disappears right after that.

Delighted with himself, Antonio returns home, on Via della Tesa, and locks himself up in his dark-room to develop the film. Red light. Deliberate conjuror's sleight of hand. Unbearable silence.

Submerged one after the other in the tanks of truth, the images soon return their verdict.

In the first image, the driver hasn't noticed; he is looking at the road, he is listening to the woman at his side who is telling him about something as she tightens the knot of the scarf around her head.

"Oh my God!"

In the second image, he is looking in the direction of the camera; he is surprised, mouth open, no doubt spouting a stream of curses; the woman at his side is also looking at the camera in open-eyed surprise, but she is still smiling.

"Oh my God, it can't be possible!"

In the last image, the man with the shaved head and racer's jumpsuit is definitely beside himself with fury: his deep black eyes are threatening and he is searching the surrounding darkness for the impudent individual who has had the gall to surprise him, just like a child who is caught red-handed. The beautiful woman at his side is no longer smiling, she has lowered her glasses onto her nose, she is unrecognizable.

It is the Duce! He is seeing Mussolini with his own eyes…

But who is that woman in the silk scarf?

He doesn't recognize her face. It is certainly not Graziosa Bocca, that young woman the Emperor met during "carnevale" and who gave him a son. No, it isn't La Sarfatti either, she whose ugliness is of as great renown as her immense fortune. And it cannot be Leda Rafanelli, either, the Duce's Oriental mistress, who wears a turban, Egyptian bracelets and heavy earrings, since the latter is a brunette.

Who on earth can it be?

Faced with these stolen images that burn his fingers, Antonio has no idea what to do. He must not show them to anyone—not even to Nora, for he does not want to compromise her. No newspaper would be willing to publish them: they are all under strict censorship. What about foreign papers? It would be an enormous risk — and Antonio is not the intrepid type.

He is then seized with a wild idea: he mails the three photos to the Duce himself in Rome, at the Palazzo Venezia. While keeping the negatives, to be sure, in a little secret strong-box, because you never know.

A week later, in the mail, is a letter from Rome, handwritten by Mussolini himself. Adopting a surprisingly familiar tone, the Duce thanks him for the images and invites him to come to Rome without delay for he would like to meet him. The letter contains a hint of admiration and not a few threats.

Just two days later, Antonio makes his appearance at the Palazzo Venezia. He is received by the Duce.

There are no images of this meeting. It will always be a missing part of this story.

No one is either to give an account of what transpired during the meeting between the two men.

When Antonio leaves the following day, after a night of feasting and roaming the streets of the capital, he is happy.

A month later, Antonio leaves Trieste for Turin with wife and child. Why this new flight? Why Turin, and not Milan, Florence, or Rome?

In Trieste, he leaves behind his two sisters and a piece of land that is not worth much.

IV

It is the end of the year. Almost Christmas. Emilie is pregnant again.

Squeezed into a much too tight skirt, breasts almost popping out of her bodice, though she is protected by a padded checkered apron secured to her chest with two safety-pins, Emilie, enormous and short of breath, drags herself from room to room, while, in the kitchen bricelets are cooking on a huge log.

Jugs of wine make their way around the tables. Small, wide-mouthed glasses are filled.

Julien is full of himself and prances around in the midst of the clients who laugh at his antics; he buys drinks for everyone to celebrate the future event. In the kitchen, the servant grumbles non- stop, Emilie chokes with anger. Pierre chases the cat with wild whoops of joy.

On a stormy October night, assisted only by a neighbor, Emilie gives birth to a baby girl. They call her Jacqueline. She is puny and her skin is purple. They have to spank her again and again before they can get her to let out that first wail.

Julien is in such a state of joy that it will be days before he sobers up.

The apartment they share above the inn is small and so run-down it is barely livable: a living- room crowded with old furniture and a single bedroom with two beds. Emilie and Julien sleep in one, the children in the other. No intimacy whatsoever. Sighs, snores, nightmares, and smothered cries of pleasure are all shared.

To everyone's surprise, Petit Pierre just adores his sister. He becomes her protector; he rocks her and feeds her; he wouldn't dream of pulling her hair. In no time, they are inseparable and when Jacqueline has a fit of anger or cries uncontrollably, Pierre is the only one who can make her stop: he takes her in his arms, lifts her up and carries her to his tricycle where, totally in charge, he sets her down with her hands on the handlebars.

The flow of tears is instantaneously stemmed. Pierre then sits behind his sister, puts his feet on the pedals and, as if by magic, the tricycle begins to move. Crisis averted! The little girl bubbles with laughter, especially when Pierre makes sounds with his mouth like a car honking.

They are never apart now. The little sister and her big brother.

She has just turned three, and he is five. They go for rides on the tricycle. They play with tops. They chase butterflies on the terrace. They try to catch trout in the basin filled with clear water. They spit in the stream. They disappear for hours without permission.

But their favorite game is to play hide-and-seek in the kitchen — Emilie's kingdom.

Behind the ovens or in the cold room, under the kitchen counters, between sacks of potatoes: a thousand hiding places to be explored with a slight shiver of fright.

Emilie waves her broom at them to drive them away. But she has no time to take care of them: the inn is full, all those sauces simmering in the pans, and impatient clients to be fed.

Their utmost delight, however, is to sneak into the kitchen in the afternoon while everyone else is taking a nap. They automatically taste anything they touch: left-over sauces, vegetable or beef broth, jars of preserves for the fruit tarts, pieces of Gruyère (Swiss cheese) marinating in wine, jams and mustard.

Sometimes, the taste is bitter and they make a face. At times it is so very bitter and disgusting that they spit it all out — right back into the pot (without ever telling anyone). Sometimes — it even makes them nauseous — they are on the verge of throwing up, so vile is the consistency or the odor. No matter how hard they try to spit it all back out, the taste of death keeps welling up in their mouth and they ruminate it until it is time for bed.

And they fall asleep, absolutely convinced that they have been poisoned.

Nevertheless, there are those irresistible, delicious aromas: some are a little tart, like cranberry jam (that goes so well with hare or roe deer) or are ecstatic, like honey from a pine tree or acacia, unexpected, like coriander leaves, misty and sweet ,like beaten egg whites, acidic, like the little cherries from the garden or rhubarb that you chew on but makes you wince, golden and crunchy, like Emilie's *bricelets*, sweetish and burning, like raisins in aquavit, suave and nauseating, like *cognarde*, a mixture of apple, pear and quince juice that is used for desserts made with preserves.

Not a day goes by that Pierre and Jacqueline haven't made up some kind of new game: ninepins, cards, records and the swing just aren't enough any more. They start cooking up plans to run away.

Pierre has a small suitcase in which he has packed a few toys, his train-master's cap and whistle, and a handful of marbles. Jacqueline has added her baby doll, a barrette for her hair and the plastic tea cups from her doll's tea set. They climbed onto the tricycle and barreled down the road all the way to the cemetery. No one noticed them.

It is the beginning of summer, perhaps the end of June, for the air is pure, transparent and the sun will burn your skin.

They followed the road all the way to Prangins. Suddenly Jacqueline felt the heat. She was tired. She was thirsty. She started to cry and couldn't stop. They abandoned the tricycle on the side of the road. They walked deep into the forest. The little girl was still crying. She was covered with perspiration.

Then, in the distance beyond the trees, they heard the sound of a stream. Pierre took his sister by the hand and they descended in wide zigzags.

When they reach the edge of the water, they feel like going in. The water is cool and not very deep. In some places, you can even see tadpoles hiding under the roots. When they enter the water, it feels funny: their feet sink into the mud and big black clouds rise to the surface. They can no longer see their feet. This makes the little sister laugh.

They decide to build a dam by piling up stones, the big ones on the bottom and smaller ones on top, cemented together with wet clay. After a while, a large pond of black water has formed and they voluptuously splash around in it. But the water continues to rise for the dam they have erected with such patience is truly impermeable.

The little girl becomes frightened. She waves her arms and she thrashes around with her legs in the sticky mud. She calls out to her brother for help. Pierre attempts to free her, but he is also a prisoner of the quicksand under his feet. With a mighty effort, he manages to pick up his sister. Once he has her in his arms, he realizes that now he, in turn, is starting to sink into the quicksand and he immediately starts screaming at the top of his lungs.

Around five o'clock in the evening, an old peasant is the one who rescues them.

Up there, in the grass, he came across the old tricycle, wheels turned up to the sky.

He searches the surroundings and then hears the screams coming from the forest.

Screams of terrified children. He scrambles down the hill. He discovers the children holding each other so closely that they have become indistinguishable, as if there were only one child. They are shaking from fear and cold.

They are pulled out of the water. The peasant lends them his shirt. Pierre and Jacqueline dry themselves, warm up a bit. They are brought home in a horse-drawn cart. With chickens in a cage, a bag of beets, and the old tricycle with its bent wheels.

Julien is waiting on the terrace, leather whip in hand.

There are children who are ghosts. They carry within themselves the memory of another world — a world beyond the forests, beyond the streams. They have bathed their bodies and their hair in the enchanted spring. That ecstasy has never left their eyes.

The little girl never quite recovered from the escapade. She becomes sad and withdrawn. She shuts herself up in the attic. She wanders around the kitchens like a ghost. Even her brother has lost the power to cheer her up. She empties the glasses of their last drops of aquavit or swallows the dregs of white wine. She burns her hands on the stoves. She knocks over dishes, pans filled with broth, cheese platters.

To punish her, they lock her up in the cellar. When they let her out, the little girl is utterly terrified, her face black with soot, her hands bloody.

One day, as she is doing a balancing act on the rim of the pond, she falls in.

She bangs her head against the stone. She has landed in the freezing water in the middle of voracious trout and carp. She loses consciousness. They carry her to the room upstairs. They wrap her up in blankets. They rub her chest with camphor oil. Julien builds a huge wood fire in the chimney.

When she regains consciousness, the little girl smiles; her eyes are shiny with fever. She mutters words that make no sense. Her little body keeps on shaking. The old doctor is at a loss. He prescribes very hot soups and mustard cataplasms. They give her a shot.

The little girl keeps smiling, but refuses to eat or drink or let them take care of her.

The following day, it is all over.

What could Pierre possibly understand when confronted with the little white coffin?

In the overflowing church the pastor spoke about glory and consolation. God in his great mercy had called Jacqueline back to Him because He loved her. Now, she was seated among the angels of Paradise. They should praise the Everlasting Lord.

Glory be to You, God of light and mercy.

Deep down, Pierre was thinking that a God who kills his children did not even deserve a prayer.

Why—if he loved her as much as he claimed — had he taken Jacqueline away from her family's love? And why punish those who loved her? What had they done to deserve such a cruel punishment?

When he passed at the foot of the great cross, Pierre stopped to look up at the Christ and addressed him in a low voice:

"If you really exist, I'll give you three minutes to strike me down. If you let me walk out of this church, it means that you don't exist!"

The inn is closed. Every night, Julien drinks until his legs buckle under his weight. On more than one occasion, a neighbor finds him in the morning, lying at the foot of a tree, next to the cemetery, open shirt and bare feet, snoring like a locomotive.

Daylight burns his eyelids. For hours on end, he just sits there in the shade, under the great plane tree on the terrace, in front of the sparkling lake. He has read the paper (only the headlines), smoked his pipe, played cards with his friends from the choral society.

Now he is dozing off, in the September sun. His eyes are burning. He can barely breathe. He is struggling to keep awake.

When he shuts his eyes, his little girl appears. She is wearing a short-sleeved cotton dress, white socks, leather sandals. She is sitting on a tricycle behind her big brother, Pierre, who is holding the handlebars. He is wearing bleached overall shorts. His feet are bare in his sandals.

The two children are pressed close together (the little girl is holding on to her brother's waist) like twins. They are both gazing in the same direction, towards Julien who suddenly sees them with horrifying clarity.

He blinks. Children screaming. Laughter. Then the tricycle is stuck in the sand.

When he opens his eyes again, only Pierre is left; he is holding the handlebars.

Julien rubs his eyes. Suddenly a hot flash suffuses his face. The ghost has passed by.

He can't believe his eyes.

Perhaps it is on this day that he lost the ability to see the world?

He opens his eyes wide. He rubs the lenses of his glasses for hours on end. He can only make out moving shadows. Spots of indistinct colors that chase after each other or blend together.

In the middle of these shadows, a little girl in a white dress.

He cannot hear her voice. He can barely make out her face — brown bangs obscuring her forehead.

On the esplanade, the big wheels of the tricycle are sucked into the mud with an unbearable screech, but the little girl laughs out loud.

While Julien is sinking into the darkness of night, Emilie is all eyes. She judges, estimates, examines, weighs, observes, and devours the world with her eyes, the better to control it.

Nothing that happens at the pub escapes her notice, nothing in the village, nothing in town. She rarely reads the papers; she listens to the radio even less, but she keeps up with all the latest by watching every move of the world.

She has always been curious, Emilie, she of the anxious, inquisitive mind.

He is always there, the secret child; invisible, mute, he floats all around the room; he soars up toward the sky; he is still howling in the little coffin that they have just put into the ground.

There are very few images from this period. Julien has thrown the camera he had bought a few years earlier from a peddler into the cellar. And Emilie has no heart for laughter or for posing in front of the small black box.

With each passing day, the number of deserters slowly grows. The pub in the center of the village has become a place to be avoided.

Julien hardly seems to notice. He is sinking into darkness and silence. He spends his time cleaning the lenses of his glasses. It isn't really to see any better. He doesn't care any more about anything that is happening around him.

Emilie stays down in the kitchen to make *malakoffs* that no one ever orders any more.

Her real life is elsewhere.

It consists of a little girl who, every night before falling asleep, holds up her arms to her for a kiss.

Those little outstretched arms, I can see them every night: they are with me as if they could travel through space and time, bodies and generations, languages and borders. It is barely an image, the ghost of an image, an aborted photo.

On certain summer nights, he drops onto a chair and just sits there, as if overcome with grief, looking up at the sky, and a star shining through the blurry mist of his tears.

Image: magic.

Almost the same word with mixed up letters.

In Julien's country, people burn them for it is a well-known fact that an image is a dangerous thing. It always betrays that which it represents. It leads to grief and death. It provokes lies and lust. It cannot be trusted.

It is black magic.

If he could erase a year of his life, it would be that accursed year of 1932!

The death of his little girl at the end of summer; the death in Geneva of Emile and Marius, massacred by the army on the evening of November 9 in front of the Palais des Expositions.

They had gone downtown to participate in the great demonstration against fascism and its leader George Oltramare, Mussolini's friend. The crowd had walked along la rue de la Croix-d'Or, then the Georges-Favon Boulevard, before reaching the plain of Plainpalais at the end of the day.

There are about four to five thousand demonstrators with trumpets and whistles just standing around in front of the hall.

Blows are exchanged with the police. Chains that had been sealed into the walls that very morning in order to contain the demonstrators, give way under the pressure.

Tension mounts. Small groups manage to isolate the soldiers. Their helmets and weapons are seized, their tunics are torn. Rifles are smashed on the sidewalks. Then the troops retreat as the mob screams:

"Go to your barracks, soldiers!"

But instead of proceeding to the Vernets barracks, the troops back up against the walls of the Palais des Expositions. The crowd has created a half-circle around the soldiers, yelling insults and throwing gravel at them; then the officer, Raymond Burnat, gave the order to shoot:

"Shoot once, aim low, fire!"

The gunfire lasts twelve seconds. It leaves 13 dead and 65 wounded.

Right after that, the crowd disperses. A deep silence falls. All those bodies left lying on the pavement.

A horrifying spectacle appears under the lights of the street-lamps.

When he sees that order has been reestablished, Burnat allows his soldiers to smoke a cigarette to break the tension.

Among the thirteen victims: Emile Guignet and Marius Rattaz, both friends of Julien's.

There are days when he wishes he could loosen the noose around his neck just a little — the past that is choking him.

No, there is no going back in time; that would be impossible and he knows it; nor can he be freed from his past; but if only he could let out the noose just a little, that his lungs be once again flooded with air, the ghosts kept at a distance.

Oh wherefore is the green grass?
In the world of memories
If my heart be flowing blood
All that flows is my face.

Whirl and spin: tops spin, spools spin, wheels spin: sorrow forever spinning around itself.

Like spinning in a dance circle. A magic trance. It denies the healing power of time and unrelenting, spins back to its beginning: a departure, death, abandonment. It celebrates without sound that which is no more.

Julien holds his breath: someone nearby, a customer, a stranger, has just pronounced the name of Jacqueline.

He is all ears. He tries to catch a few words. He lies in wait for long moments.

Words are ghosts who travel from mouth to mouth, from ear to ear. They carry both terror and joy. They kindle sorrow. They ignite desire. They are messengers of all that we have lost. They are the echoes of our loves. Words allow us, if only for an instant, to recover all the faces we have loved and who have left us behind.

"Jacqueline."

Like images, language is magic. It can reach deep within us and touch raw flesh, that intimate and secret part of us upon which time has no hold.

"Jacqueline."

Words seep into that wound (ears forever straining to hear) that we endeavor, as best we can, to keep to ourselves.

"Jacqueline."

They seem to enjoy blowing on open wounds. Yet we love words, for we cherish our wounds.

Ever since the little girl's death, Emilie spends all her time doing laundry.

First she brings up the wood to a small room on the first floor that is used as a laundry room.

In the evening, when she comes home after work, she lights a big fire to heat up the water, to let the laundry soak. The following day, she washes. The third day, she rinses and hangs up the laundry to dry.

The inn is never quite clean enough. The floor must be mopped, the wood floor of the family room must be waxed, the glasses made to sparkle, the pots and pans scrubbed till they shine and she is never done...

Any remaining energy, Emilie uses up by tracking down dirt and traces of grease. She soundlessly drags her fatigue behind her; she works herself to death; this is her way of making amends.

The sleepy inn, bathed in sunlight; the grey of the cinderblock, the yellow of the grass on the pond stones, the blue of the lake wrinkled by currents like an old parchment, and the tricycle with its bent wheels, a silver stain on the terrace.

The red of Julien's eyes: he is under the great chestnut tree rubbing the lenses of his glasses with the utmost care.

Nose buried in his mother's skirts: his mother who in turn kisses and scolds and then kisses again, his mother in an apron who lets him lick the copper bowl still warm and sticky from the currant jelly; his mother who, all of a sudden, grabs hold of him and crushes his head between her enormous breasts and chants the name of a little girl, over and over again, very softly as if in a foreign language.

How long did they remain in that empty inn where still burns the image of their little girl? Six months, or perhaps a year.

When one day they finally packed up, it was for good and without regrets.

The villagers did not express any regrets either. And they let them leave for the city without saying a word. This is how the Vaudois are: in a hurry to forget what was part of their lives and that they loved for so long.

V

Once again, Nora is pregnant.

"It'll be a boy!" trumpets Antonio from every rooftop.

It's a girl. They call her Pierrette.

Turin, 1930. All of a sudden, life takes off and explodes. The Duce's recommendation allows Antonio to become a member of *L'Unione Cinematografica Educativa*[1] (the famous LUCE) founded by Mussolini in 1924.

For nearly twenty years, LUCE will produce all of the regime's propaganda images, including cinema, photography or simply graphic arts. Films, photos, postcards, banners, stamps, decorations, decals for decorating cups, letterhead stationery, *fumetti* (comic strips) will endlessly reproduce the retouched portrait of the Duce.

Simple employee to begin with, it isn't long before, given his artistic talents, Antonio begins to rapidly climb the rungs of the Luciferian hierarchy. A hard worker, oblivious to the number of sleepless nights, he will always be positively reviewed by his superiors (who are, however, wary of his original ideas). He travels extensively, from Rome to Trieste, from Florence to Venice, from Lucca to Sorrento; nevertheless, he closely monitors every step of the image production.

First, the touch-ups, which might just mean being mindful of etiquette. The object being to erase any *faux pas*, any slight appearance of ridicule, any misunderstanding or mistaken identity, or just random *trompe-l'oeil* images. For in every image, there is always something not quite right, or weird, or worrisome: it might be a hat left behind in a random place, an important personality who isn't where he is supposed to be, an out-of-place object (umbrella, telescope, cigarette butt, bottle of wine) that might be distracting.

Any one of these might turn the photo into something trivial: it has to be retouched.

To this end, Antonio advocates a return to an artistic soft-focus, to the glamour of Hollywood portraits. Shadows are barely masked. The grain of the skin disap-

---

1 The Union for Educational Cinema.

pears. Faces float in front of a uniform background, deprived of reference, a sort of dusky void that elevates them.

Then, as it rises against a gray and dull sky, surrounded by a dreamlike halo, the portrait of the Emperor becomes iconic and acquires eternal youth.

But sometimes just retouching is not enough and further work must be done. The central character (that never changes) is then skillfully outlined and everything else that might be a problem is erased: background settings, secondary characters, pedestrian objects.

The orders Antonio received were simple, but they often changed. He was required to erase a certain official personality who had become *persona non grata*. He was also required to erase (and the Duce himself made sure of this) any unattractive woman who appeared in the image. Not out of any aesthetic concern, but because the Emperor was of necessity handsome and therefore could generate only beauty in his wake.

For the tyrant is untouchable. That he might be soiled by pedestrian objects or personalities of no significance is unthinkable. He is the solitary hero: the One and Only.

An intense void protects his sacred body, like a halo of divine light.

Sometimes a perfect image necessitates the bringing together of two personalities who are far apart or who belong to two separate photos.

Just like children playing with scissors and paper, Antonio cuts out a paper figure, removes it from its base and places it in a new setting. Then, like a painter organizing the elements of his canvas, he composes the image he wishes to create.

It is an exciting game — the work of a poet. But dangerous as well. Proportions must be observed, traces of touch ups, shadows that don't belong, as well as variations in the grain or thread of the paper must be erased; incongruous mingling of genres must be avoided. Gestures and glances must coincide. The angle of the light must be the right one. The new image must be as ordinary and coherent as possible.

What is the meaning of photography?

It means to cut out a window on reality.

It is the freest of actions, but the most arbitrary as well. For this open window is enclosed by frames. These are what limits and conditions the image. Certain objects or certain beings are within the frame — others are not.

This is the very essence of art: reality never appears in its totality. The dictator, in this case, is the eyes of the photographer.

You might say that each image that is published, republished, cut out, and cut out again, exists with its successive layers of "outside the frame," like peeling an onion.

From the moment of its conception, like God himself, the photographer continually reframes his creation.

In the middle of the night, a phone call.

"Campo? You have to rub out Starace!"

This is how, in their secret language, the Duce expresses himself.

This or that personality, even yesterday the crowd's darling and looked upon with favor in Rome, has fallen into disgrace. It could be anyone: a minister turned arrogant, a counselor to the Prince, a mistress turned a bit too needy.

"Rub out Starace!"

As soon as he hangs up, Antonio gets to work and erases the intruder from all the official images. Armed with a pocket knife, he cuts a slit in the setting through which he skillfully makes the undesirable one disappear. Secret tomb. A forgotten page in history books. Communal grave of anonymous heroes. Then, like a surgeon, he sutures the edges. In order to make the scar undetectable, he uses black and white gouache and he follows the original shades. Little by little, textures and shapes cover up the eliminated characters.

Sublime paintbrush strokes that send off the arrogant, the ambitious, the parvenus to eternal dust.

How many ghosts in these walls?

These half-opened doors, unfurled flags, abruptly empty stands, patched up tapestries, touched up mirrors?

In his laboratory, Antonio (aka Campo) holds absolute power: as if by magic, child's play, he eliminates, liquidates, erases, and causes the disappearance of physical bodies and restores eternal youth to those faces that appear in full light.

Turin is a city of tunnels and secret passages. Even when it is raining, you can traverse it in every direction without being touched by a single drop of water. For dandies, it is a paradise and for elegant women, certain ruin: luxury stores give way to jewelry stores, trilingual bookshops to specialty grocery stores, beauty shops to high-end leather-goods stores.

Without even realizing it or setting foot outside, you have walked around the entire city, from the Piazza Castello to the Carignano Theatre, by way of the Porta Nuova Train Station and the grandiose Piazza della Repubblica.

Nora just loves her new city, and so does her daughter, Livia.

For her sixth birthday, her father has given her a tricycle with rubber-covered wheels. And Livia is off at top speed, under the tall luminous arcades while Nora, gasping for breath, runs behind her.

For Antonio, this marks the beginning of madness. He travels extensively, makes the rounds of innumerable official dinners, rubs elbows with the state's highest ranked personalities, and is courted by the most beautiful women in Italy.

During the day, armed with his Leica, he shoots away at the upper crust, and at night, in his laboratory, with broad brush strokes, scissors and glue, he gives shape to this new man, the legionnaire of modern Italy, the Duce's great dream: dynamic, virile, determined, prepared to make any sacrifice, hardened by a spartan education.

Venice, Florence, Amalfi, Sorrento, Lucca: wherever the Emperor goes as he travels throughout Italy, Antonio goes with him, like an invisible double. He multiplies the images, he accumulates proofs, he hunts down evidence.

At times, his photos appear in *Life* or *Epoca*, with captions glorifying the Duce. For example, this very glamorous image where he is seen kissing Louise Brooks (the first silver screen *femme fatale*) in a flannel coat adorned with a fox collar and sleeves with cutwork sable fur: that was the day, it would seem, that the Emperor truly met his match!

Images are what Antonio brings back from everywhere: there are those of the Emperor and his entourage (which often changes for the man is temperamental and distrusts courtiers,) the official photographs of the meetings with Hitler or Franco (whom he considers with contempt), and then the others, all of the others, with the mistresses for a day, where you can see him ski, pilot a motorboat, dive into a heart-shaped pool. These images are by far the most numerous, for the Duce loves to show off his athletic body. He is proud of his muscles, of his clean-shaven head. He loves this impression of virile strength which he gives off.

This is the hero he wishes Italians to see: Hercules with a body sculpted by working out, looking stern, while he directs his inexorable gaze far beyond any obstacle towards the final victory.

In his opinion, a successful image is a face where there are no shadows. A smooth and burnished visage, spotless and unlined: it is a visage without a wrinkle.

Night after night, he cuts out. He outlines. He smoothes over. He reframes. He erases. He eliminates secrets. He works in obscurity, but it is exhilarating. As if, with each reworked image, he were giving a new birth to his idol.

Through his handiwork, the Emperor is reborn, more handsome, more vigorous, and most of all as the bearer of a brighter light.

It is summer. Heat lies heavy on the empty streets.

Nora takes her enormous paunch for a walk under the arcades in search of a little cool air.

Twenty meters ahead of her, Livia on her tricycle follows the arabesques traced on the ground.

"This time, I want a boy!" Antonio issues, like an ultimatum.

It will be a girl, the third, who will be called Elvire and who will become a world champion figure skater.

That same summer, while he is swimming across the Po river, indistinguishable in the midst of accomplished swimmers, Mussolini is carried away by the current. The crowd, assembled on the riverbanks applauds and shouts. Antonio is the only one who has the courage to throw himself in pursuit and, in the backwash catches up with him and pulls him to shore.

As of that day, in order to avoid competition from his party comrades, all of them excellent swimmers, the Duce decides he will swim alone, far removed from currents, in a place where the water is not deep — but he will invite all the press members to witness his exploits.

Antonio is always nearby with his Leica at the ready, to immortalize the scene and create the legend of a half-god who dominates fate and all its vicissitudes…

In this city known for its fog and black masses, Campo will craft the legend of the Duce.

It is multifaceted and its faces — like those of Proteus — are countless: first, we are shown the tireless worker who is able to spend ten to fifteen hours in his office (a light burns all night in the window facing Piazza Venezia), who will digest mountains of files, hold meeting upon meeting with his ministers as well as countless interviews with diplomats — all without a pause, except once in a while, for a glass of milk with a little bread and cheese.

Countless are the times Campo will immortalize this scene: the Emperor seated at his Spartan desk, dipping his pen in a bronze inkwell, all his pencils neatly placed in a small porcelain vase with a flower design, left elbow resting on the blotter, dark eyes riveted on a small miniature of his mother, Rosa Mussolini.

Not to forget the crowd haranguer standing on his podium, chin jutting forward, a Luciferian look on his face, ready to switch roles from one second to the next according to his mood or the cries of the crowd, waxing at times lyrical and at others menacing, rolling his eyes and invoking the heavens as witness.

Every time he can, Campo emphasizes the theatrical gesture, the flamboyant settings, as well as the solitude of the character, a lone figure facing the crowds, playing up his talents as an actor, alternating long periods of chanting in a powerful voice with tirades in *mezzo voce,* shock formulas with provocative gestures.

Miracle of photography: a short man with a shaved head, nothing more than a performing street acrobat, acquires thus the stature of a God!

One day, it is the summer of 1933, a phone call.

"Campo, come right away! We are going to the seashore"!

Antonio obeys, he has no choice, he rushes to the Palazzo Venezia with a suitcase filled with his equipment.

The Duce is waiting for him seated at the wheel of his red Alfa: he is wearing aviator glasses, race-car driver jump-suit, black leather gloves. With a look of defiance, he is about to challenge all the gods of speed: he is the new man, master of technology and time; nothing can resist him.

It is autumn, a gay and multi-colored autumn. Nora takes her daughters for a walk along the Po. There are three of them, now: Livia is eight, Pierrette six, and Elvire four. They all wear the fascist uniform. The two younger ones fight over the tricycle. The older sister tries to separate them. Nora feels weary in her muslin dress.

Night falls. From the river rises a yellow mist that swallows up all the luxurious villas, one after the other. The wild hills have become invisible. It is almost impossible to make out the arches of a bridge. The chestnut trees are ghosts filled with birds.

Turin: the secret child will always associate this city with summer vacation. We would arrive in summer at the Porta Nuova Train Station; Antonio, with his fine mustache and felt hat, looking like an English aristocrat, would be waiting for us on the track where the train came in. He would pick up our suitcases. A brisk walk across town and then we would reach the Via Susa apartment.

Nora would hold out her arms and embrace us. She had prepared cups of steaming hot chocolate and *fritelle*, these fritters of dough covered with confectioner's sugar. Antonio would play the harmonium. We would watch *Carosello* on the old black and white TV and we would smoke Antonio's cigarettes (MS filters) when he wasn't looking.

Those were the most wonderful summer vacations in the world.

The war had been over for twenty years.

Surely no man in all of history has ever made use of such extraordinary means to ensure his visibility at every instant, at every sequence of his life!

We witness him playing the violin, fencing, diving, shooting a rifle, harvesting or blacksmithing in public. At every event, he is followed by a swarm of photographers — amongst which Campo, of course, who never misses an iota of this spectacle.

First, he is an actor who dresses up as a peasant, a laborer, a fireman, a *bersagliere*, a deep-sea diver, an aviator, a miner, a fearless horseman. He has no reticence when it comes to making a great show of himself in swimming attire or bare chested. He has no end of increasingly wild head-gear ranging from gas mask to top-hat, from bowler hat to fascist fez, from American baseball cap to colonial helmet.

In the eyes of the Italian people, he is the very model of courage, of heroic work, of boundless virility; he is a superman exercising body and mind to the limits, the fighter, always prepared to return to combat.

At the time, in every corner of Italy, schoolchildren draw portraits of the Emperor in the purist "futuristic" style so dear to Marinetti. A style imbued with the simple and geometric shapes of modernity.

Antonio's daughters are no exception: just like every schoolchild their own age, there is no end to the competitive display of skills when it comes to drawing with colored pencils or painting with gouache the impassive face of a Roman emperor, sometimes topped by an eagle with menacing wings, sometimes astride his ceremonial horse.

In a corner of the image, instead of the signature and in its place, you will find the inscription DUX which looks like Roman numerals and is also found on the base of busts or on columns, often in symmetry with the analogous inscription REX (since the real king of Italy is not the "little king" Victor-Emmanuel, but is in fact this character who has been head of state for the past twelve years, and who, each day, invents new images to glorify himself.)

All of these glorious images, Livia, just like millions of Italians, has carried them in her innermost being since early childhood. They have grown within her, they have branched out and have borne miraculous and invisible fruit. They will always be associated with childhood. They will in fact become the very essence of her own childhood and the last resort, an imaginary one, when the world will betray her desires.

It is a treasure-chest of pious images, inscribed on the wax of memory, that she is able to read at any time, eyes shut, heart overcome by emotion: the appeal to the imaginary Father, to the highest Authority, to the supreme Guide who knows the way and who will protect her from all the pitfalls of the world.

A tyrant's secret — Livia will think many years later — is to reign through images. Not just any images: those images inscribed during childhood. This is the place, this treasure of unconscious effigies, living, indestructible, from which he draws the essential core of his powers. These images, outside of time, are the foundation of his fascination.

But childhood is not eternal. In order for this fascination to last, there is only one way: that childhood never end, that it might be prolonged to last throughout one's entire lifetime. The child must never grow up. Even as an adult, he must remain a child. Even when he is about to draw his last breath, he must remain infant: he who has not yet been given the right to a voice, who obeys, who admires without understanding, who lives and acts under the influence of these images.

This is the reason the Master — whether he be called Mao, Stalin, Hitler or Mussolini — constantly infantilizes the crowds of his adoring fans (just as he demonizes his detractors.) It is only at this cost that he is able to establish his authority.

Childhood begins with images. Only an aberration could lead mankind to believe that he can apprehend the world in its simplicity and its reality, the way it really is, whenever since earliest childhood he has only been able to perceive misleading reflections, echoes, muted, uncertain, filled with lacunae.

Childhood feeds on phantoms: faces without voice and voices without faces, unfamiliar glances, mysterious words, shapes and colors that never delineate anything substantial, but instead are the halo of a central absence.

An idolatrous nation is one intoxicated with images: this is no doubt what the Emperor has grasped from the early period of his coming to power, before any of his political adversaries. This is why, at every stage of his glorious ascent, he multiplies the icons of himself: top hat (his detractors call it stove-pipe), starched wing collar, bourgeois suit as befits the man who has restored order; and then he is shown as the intrepid equestrian, otter skin cap and condottiere uniform, adopting the posture of the Roman Caesars (at the bottom of the photograph you can read the following inscription: if I move forward, follow me. If I retreat, kill me); then, cranium protected by a helmet, a faraway look on his face, determined jaw, in the uniform of an honorary corporal of the militia; and finally, hatless, head clean-shaven in the style, of Erich von Stroheim, determined expression, jaw jutting forward, adopting the look of the soldier inured to the rigors of self-sacrifice. And that is how he will reign over Italy as absolute tyrant for more than twenty years—thanks to the fascination of images.

In this delirium of masks and exaggerated postures, Campo has a role to play. He selects the negatives, crops them cleverly or resets them. Through the magic of collage, armed with glue and scissors, he creates an association between the silhouette of the Duce and the Colosseum, for example, or the now miraculously erect Tower of Pisa. He recreates a new mythology: that of the solitary lion.

"As long as I have a pen in my hand and a revolver in my pocket, I fear no one. I am strong, even though I am almost alone. I would almost say that I am strong precisely because I am alone."

Throughout all those years in the workshops of Milan, Trieste, Turin, and Rome, Campo works at the universal mastery of light (the Eden-like name *LUCE* which is Italian for light).

Shadows are hunted down, and then erased from every image, just as the enemy inside is arrested, sent to prison or even executed.

And in the image, henceforth, everything becomes visible: no more secrets, no more margins or dangerous blurred elements.

Light reigns as absolute mistress

Even if, for almost ten years, he is the *œil* of the Emperor, Antonio does not see everything.

Never will he participate in the punitive expeditions organized by the brownshirts against the labor councils or trade unionists. And never will he be even a witness to these atrocities. First, the headquarters were sacked and set on fire. Then, the leaders were hunted down and savagely beaten with *manganellos* (phallic cudgel of punitive action).

Finally, faces and bodies a bloody mess, they were forced to drink castor oil that would immediately make them vomit. They were then abandoned in their own excrement, unless, without even a trial, they were shot on the spot with a bullet to the head.

Antonio's happiness (for I imagine Antonio happy) is to collate images.

His dream? To make images and time coincide.

It matters not which images: the truthful and the truncated, those deemed appropriate for public consumption and the secret ones, the solemn and the frivolous, the silent, the voluble, the obscure, the glorious, the damned.

How many images discarded as a sacrifice to the changes wrought by the passage of time!

And how many present moments have been magnified, how many unresolved enigmas and how many revelations does he offer us in these images purloined from History, images that today shine with unsurpassed daring!

Like a privileged witness, Campo records both shadow and light, the heroic face of the horseman or of the pilot able to rise above the meanness of the world and the pettiness of the flock, but he records as well the dark side of the dictator, tired or sick, grimacing in pain as he clutches his stomach with both hands, the unfaithful husband; the broken tennis player after a lost match, the diplomat multiplying clandestine meetings.

These secret images, Campo has hundreds of them, but he shows them to no one. He safeguards them in a wooden strong-box in the living-room of the large Turin apartment.

Nora knows nothing of this

Only Livia, one day, has seen him slip something, furtively, under the floor-boards.

Every image secretes a secret.

How many censored images does Campo possess in his treasure?

There are all the mistresses (the one night stands or the ones who lasted a week): la Rafanelli, wearing only an oriental turban, offering — as if on a dish — her breasts to the Emperor who is in ecstasy; la Dalser, bejeweled and powdered, eyes drunk with love; la Bocca who is playing with a carnival mask; la Sarfatti, looking sad and empty as she readjusts her bra-strap; la Petacci, her hair dripping with soap, perched on high heels, naked as a new-born babe. And hordes of the anonymous ones, the regional beauties, the hysterical, the silent, and the enamored, the garrulous ones, the arrogant (since fascism, after all, for the majority of Italians, is a story of love).

A little further, in a large envelope, there are all the secret meetings, the dealings with Churchill, a longtime admirer of the Duce, the late evening meetings with Franco, Goering, Laval, Chamberlain, Dollfus, the tête-à-têtes with the little king of Italy, and the hushed meetings with the pope.

But the most dangerous images, without a doubt, are those that show the other face of the Emperor: the creased wrinkles of fatigue, the rictus of an all too human pain, the look of weakness and neglect, the forced smiles, the eyes suddenly filled with fright, the mouth that spits blood and the sickly complexion of a hero weakened by purges and vomiting: the mask of depression.

The following morning at teatime, the mask has disappeared. Here is a man in great shape, radiating good health, and pointing at a map of Africa with his finger

"Abyssinia will be ours! The country of our ancestor…"

As Campo stares at him wide-eyed, the dictator fires up.

"Extraordinary, isn't it? I, Mussolini, will bring battalions across the desert! I at the head of the Leoni, I will hunt the small Negus.

Rolling his eyes:

"Africa has always belonged to us"

Then at the height of enthusiasm:

"First Africa, then Asia…"

And finally, as if the wave that had carried him to the height of ecstasy had abruptly collapsed.

"We are living a glorious age, wouldn't you agree Campo? I am proud to participate in this new energy…

Turin, for Nora, is the city of fancy balls, large banquets, and evenings at the Carignano Theatre.

She is expecting a child, but she does not know it yet. She is dancing in the arms of Antonio — in his gala uniform — who has just been appointed *cavaliere*. She is wearing a black, tulle dress that sets off her bare shoulders, sapphire earrings and a double strand pearl necklace.

She is also becoming intoxicated by the lights of power, but she is careful not to burn her wings. She prefers the days spent with her daughters, the walks along the banks of the Po, and Sunday picnics on the hill of Superga.

Photo session at the Palazzo Venezia.

The Emperor, who has gotten rid of his puma, has just received a female lion cub as a gift. It terrorizes the domestic help, pisses all over the rugs, sharpens its claws on the antique furniture, and lets fly terrifying roars. He christens her Italia on the spot and takes a liking to the animal, identifying with it, as he boasts of his bestial flair and his insatiable appetite.

"Meglio vivere un giorno da leone che cento da pecora!" (Better to live one day as a lion than a hundred as a sheep!)

They are there, face to face in the living room of the great Roman palace, the son of a blacksmith from Romagna and his iconographer, the son of the director of the Evangelical School of Trieste. The one who has brutally seized Italy, without qualms, the way you would seduce a middle-class maiden pining for romantic love or an adolescent girl you had come upon in Rimini at a beauty pageant; the one who has tamed her, over the years, who thrust his Boot on her boot by imposing a regimen of work on his fellow citizens (the first and only Italian Statesman—as they gloat about it in the North—who has managed to make Sicilians work); the one who dreams of Abyssinia and military conquests, and one who has reduced his fierce political adversaries to silence, one after the other.

And facing him, hidden behind the tripod of his camera, well within reach of sword or whip, the little photographer, who is aware that he is important, but does not know why, the one who measures light and organizes the dramatic setting with meticulous attention that borders on the obsessive (the bust of Caesar on the light-colored fireplace mantle, the wild beast asleep at the Emperor's feet, the tricolor flag as background). He observes his model. He notices that the tie is crooked and that the wing collar is not straight, that the skull is shining with unsightly reflections. A dictator owes it to himself to be impeccable. He straightens out the tie, whether it be red or blue is of no importance: the photos are in black and white. He aligns the folds of the wing collar. He lightly powders the cranium, freshly shaved that is shining like glass.

Silence.

No more breathing.

Posterity is watching us.

Antonio's finger is about to release the shutter.

Light is shining through the window, a yellow and blue late autumn light. The city is buzzing behind the window panes, but we cannot hear it. We are in the silence of frozen Time. Through the curtains, the sky appears colorless, minuscule and crumpled. The Emperor is becoming impatient.

"Are you done, Campo?"

"Not yet, Monsieur. I would like to take advantage of this beautiful light to take more pictures."

"I have work to do, Campo."

"For once, Italy can wait."

The Emperor resumes the pose, impassive and docile. He slips his right hand onto his stomach through the opening of his waistcoat of purple and yellow silk facings. He suppresses a grimace of pain. He turns his face away. He sneezes.

"Oh! These damned flowers."

There are carnations and sweet peas on the desk, among the stacks of documents, as well as bunches of jasmine in crystal vases that are brightened and burned by the light, as they exhale overdone and nauseating smells.

"Be still now!"

Silence, once again

As before, the Emperor holds his breath.

Who is dominating whom in this silent, face-to-face confrontation?

Which of the two is staging the other? The Emperor of Italy or the master of Time?

The photographer knows he is powerful, but at the same time an instrument of fate and unaccountable, he does not bring his power into play. He is an artist. History has no hold on him. His images are worth gold and he knows it, as he knows they are worth less today than tomorrow. They will soon be on the front pages of the newspapers from Rome to Berlin, from Turin to Moscow, from Treviso to Paris, and from London to Timbuktu. And everyone will be fighting over them.

From the silent *tete-a-tetes* in the jasmine-fragranced living room, who will emerge the victor?

The hunter or his prey? The photographer or his model?

It is a latent duel, devious and grueling, a strange copulation where bodies do not touch, the eyes take stock of each other from a distance, exchanged words ricocheting like bullets.

Body to body, without contact, a skirmish of words like blunted swords. A stealthy altercation.

Every time, out of every one of these intimate meetings without witnesses, images are born.

Like a midwife, Antonio is required to bring strong images into the world, images that are rooted in time and space, but at the same time are eternal, sacred and mythical. He must make the hidden body appear. He has to use forceps to aid the birth and rid it of all its mortal attributes, its temporary rags, its tics and mannerisms, and any of its contingent desires.

He brings his own father into the world.

What is a myth?

It is a word (or an image) pertaining to origin.

Not an image (or a word) that would have made its way to us from an origin, that would have traveled through time, as if by miracle, without suffering its ravages, that would carry origin in its core: luminous, intact and transparent. But instead a word (an image) that would possess the strength and value of origin, that would come to occupy the place of origin, a place that is always missing.

Myth is Antonio's field of operation. Myth is what he is attempting to construct at each one of these meetings with the Duce. He invents images of origin: the Empire Builder, the outstanding Sportsman, the *Pater Familias,* the Haranguer of crowds, the Pure and Dauntless Pilot.

Whether he is in military uniform, bare-chested, or informally dressed with Donna Rachele and the children, the photographer must call forth the mythical figure, the sacred and eternal body, the icon or archetype that all Italian (and especially Italian women) passionately embrace as a model. Not only because every mythical figure is an authority figure (since it is a figure of origin), but also because of a narcissistic phenomenon: by adoring an image of origin, crowds are fully involved, and through their active participation, they see themselves become part of the Myth.

What is a photograph?

It is but an instant of truth, a mute ravishing, a rape in broad daylight of a soul and a body.

Only the body is visible. It takes up the entire space with its carnality, its impenetrable massive bulk. However, the soul is definitely present; it bursts through the frozen screen of silver bromide. It burns out. It radiates. Only ashes remain.

Rome, Sunday afternoon.

In his studio, a stone's throw from the Trevi Fountain, Antonio is taking a little nap. He has spent the entire night in his dark room, developing, making enlargements, refining and putting the finishing touches by hand on the dozens of photos taken the day before at the Palazzo Venezia that are to be distributed the following day to the newspapers in Italy as well as throughout all of Europe.

And now he is resting, sprawled on the living-room sofa, a glass of genipi liqueur in hand. But the telephone rings.

"Campo?"

"Sì, signorsì!"

"I would require your assistance concerning an urgent matter."

"Which matter, Sir?"

"I will explain. See you tonight. At the arena. Come alone."

An hour later, they meet in front of the gates of the Coliseum. The Emperor is not alone, but surrounded by two stooges who look somber and mysterious. One of them is holding a large scabbard, the other a leather briefcase stuffed with documents.

"Come, Campo."

The Duce takes his little photographer aside, leads him to a secluded spot under an arch and suddenly lowers his voice.

"You have to do me a favor, Campo."

"Gladly, Sir. What can I do for you?"

The Emperor stares at him with unwavering black eyes.

"You are going to fight a duel."

"I beg your pardon, Sir?"

"Yes, Campo. You need to take my place to settle a small dispute."

"Which dispute, Sir?"

"A Neapolitan lawyer who is accusing me of having knocked up his wife."

"Is it the truth, Sir?"

"What can I say, Campo. The shrew burst into my office like an English cannonball: she threw herself at my feet, begged me for my autograph. Which I gave her, of course. That wasn't enough for her. She ripped open her shirt and exposed her chest to me as she kept repeating: 'Sign me, *per favore!* Sign me everywhere!' Which I did, Campo."

"Much to your credit, Sir."

"Thank you, Campo."

"And then?"

"Things began to get somewhat out of hand. I can't remember. But one thing led to another and I affixed my stamp a little bit everywhere on this young person, and something else as well, in such a way that..."

"That?"

"That she is expecting triplets. And her husband (an irascible Neapolitan) has challenged me to a sword fight. But I cannot fight, Campo."

"And why would that be, Sir?"

"Italy, Campo. Italy! I cannot run the risk of turning her into an orphan. This is why I have turned to you. Kill this man for me."

"But, Sir…"

"There are no buts, Campo. Otherwise I will feed you to my lion."

The tone leaves no room for discussion, the look somber, the lip curled in a snarl.

With the same pace, both men enter the Coliseum. The witnesses are already gathered, in the middle of the arena, together with the wronged husband wrapped in a black cape. The night is clear and aromatic. It is a clear and fragrant night. Campo chooses his sword with great care, checks the edge of the blade, the balance of the pommel. He has not fenced in months. But he, too, is just as loath to turn Livia, Pierrette, and Elvire into orphans.

They count ten steps. The two adversaries salute each other, then the witnesses give the signal for the duel to begin. Fortunately, the sparring does not last long. After throwing himself at his opponent in a furious attack, the cuckold loses his balance, is taken by surprise when Antonio dodges, slices into thin air and falls flat on his face into the dust.

Upon rising back up to his feet, he finds a sword at his throat.

"Long live the Duce!" he mumbles, seething with rage, before laying down his arms.

But the Emperor is long gone. He was picked up by a black Alfa Romeo; at the wheel, a young woman with platinum blonde hair, blue raincoat, sunglasses and who looks like a Hollywood star. The limousine blasts off towards Ostia in a cloud of dust. The Emperor was not to be found for two entire days.

Only once, did he cross swords with the Emperor.

It was in Taormina, April 1936, at the peak of his glory.

It is late afternoon as they are arriving from Rome. In the first limousine, the Emperor in the full uniform of the Honorary Corporal of the Militia—gray-green jacket and riding breeches, wide leather belt, shoulder strap and black fez. In the second limo, the indomitable Edda (who has left her Capri art nouveau palace for the day) and her husband, Count Ciano who has just been named minister of Foreign Affairs. In the third car, Giuseppe Bottai and Achille Starace, the two highest ranking members of the regime; they absolutely detest each other, but the Emperor takes malicious pleasure in taking them both with him every time he goes on a trip. Whereas Bottai is considered the party's *intellectual* — which, in everyone's eyes, is far from a compliment — due to his knowledge of the Futurist movement and his magazine *Critica Fascista* in which he advocates dropping violence and setting up an ethical State. "Starace the terrible," in contrast, is the inventor of the *fascist style* that requires Italians to substitute the formal *Lei* with the popular *Voi* in everyday language; he who has introduced the goose-step in military parades, prohibits the drinking of coffee and even blames *pastasciutta* for making the Italian race dangerously soft.

Zigzagging between the elegant limousines, Leica slung over his shoulder, Antonio attempts as best he can to keep his balance on a powerful Bianchi motorcycle driven by a quarrelsome pilot in a mask who runs the bike gunned at full throttle.

The drive up to the town is anything but pleasant. The road winds around itself in dizzying curves, becoming increasingly narrow, running at every moment precariously close to the precipice. Campo shuts his eyes and chews on a licorice stick to keep from puking.

When they reach the foot of the belvedere, the convoy slows down. Campo opens his eyes again. Up there, the Taormina citadel rises straight as an arrow, beautiful and unapproachable, from the middle of the clouds.

Another stop in front of the Messina door. The officials step out of the vehicles in strict hierarchical order: the Emperor first, then his dauphin, Ciano, and lastly, the ministers. The mayor, a small man with a sly smile, symbolically offers the keys to his town to the Duce, then the procession sets out on foot for the Greek amphitheater where the tiers are already swarming with people gathered for this event.

A cold and salty wind blows in from the sea, carrying swirls of sand in its path. On the tiers as well as on the podium, all are doing their utmost to protect themselves against the onslaught. The mayor steps forward, with his thinning tuft of yellow hair, speech in hand, shouts his head off to be heard, but the wind rips the pages out of his hand. The little man is forced to concede defeat and to retreat.

It is now the Emperor's turn: forehead held high, eyes deep and close-set, square chin, quivering lips. He begins to speak in the turmoil of the storm and, like a mime, he makes faces to emphasize each part of his speech, which immediately earns him the crowd's favor. Very few gestures. Roving and implacable eyes. At times, he stuffs both hands in his pockets. It is his "statue" moment. Then both his arms whirl above his head. Fingers become restless. The words spring forth in cascades from his lips. A moment later, he is still again. He frowns. With two fingers, he adjusts the collar of his uniform.

When it starts raining, the orator raises his fist to the sky, more threatening than ever. But the rain doesn't stop. Just the opposite, a shower of hailstones soon descends upon the tiers of the old Greek theatre. It is a free-for-all. Each one seeks shelter wherever he can, while the Emperor, stunned, continues to speak, eyes glowering, imperious and definitive gestures. Even the officials, even Ciano and the indomitable Edda, even the faithful Bottai and Starace, they have all fled to find shelter under an arch of the amphitheater.

Only Antonio, silent and stoic, eye glued to his camera, has remained in the arena to immortalize this pathetic moment: the dictator, lone forgotten figure on the podium haranguing an empty theatre under a shower of hailstones as big as currants.

That evening, despite a warm bath and several glasses of milk and honey (as a way to manifest the extent of his foul mood, he will have refused to attend the official dinner and to even taste the sumptuous *antipasti* (appetizers) prepared in his honor, refusing as well a glass of the famous fresh and delicious liqueur made with lemon pulp (called *limoncello*), the Emperor is beside himself with rage.

The sack of the royal suite assigned to him at the San Domenico will not suffice to calm him down. He tosses out the window a Piedmontese clock, a couple of Ming vases, and those well-known images of lascivious adolescents, crowned with laurels, posing against a pasteboard background, Arcadia or Cythère, by Wilhelm von Gloeden at the end of the previous century.

In fear of retaliation, Edda and her husband have left the palace and have made their way back down to the coast to seek out a gambling casino. Bottai has fled to the Public Gardens to read. As for Starace, he has barricaded himself in his room, a pistol under his pillow.

And now, the Emperor is demanding two swords, which a terrified maid leaves in front of his door.

"Someone bring a man to me! If there are any real men left in this town…"

There is only one man to be found: slumped in an armchair in the reception area, unshaven, camera straps around his neck almost garrotting him; it is Antonio. They wake him up. Someone pushes him into the elevator. Half-asleep, he knocks at the Emperor's door.

"Enter!"

When they come face to face, the Master, sword in hand, and the little photographer armed with his Leica, they are both startled.

"Well then, Campo, the last man left would be you?

"*Si, Signorsi.*"

The room is in an indecent state of chaos, as if it had been ransacked by more than a dozen burglars. The windows with their broken panes, swing back and forth uselessly on empty space. There are no more vases on the dressers, nor are there paintings left on the walls. A bunch of old photos, ashes still swirling all the way up to the high ceiling, has not quite finished burning in the hearth.

"What happened, Sir?

"Nothing, Campo. Tonight I feel like killing a man."

Antonio utters not a word. The Emperor throws him one of the two swords. "*En garde* Signor photographer!"

Campo has no time to rid himself of his old gear: the Emperor descends upon him, with a lunge, aiming high. Antonio dodges but barely in time. The other loses his balance, gets up again, then rushes back in attack mode. Antonio takes one step aside. Taken by surprise, the Emperor goes for the *quinte* and runs an armchair through.

"*Porca Madonna!*"

And now they are facing each other, the photographer and his model, the artist and the tyrant, the public figure and the anonymous one, like two irascible scoundrels. They cross swords with a roar. Foaming at the mouth. Eyes blinded.

Neither one will come out unscathed, no matter how the duel ends, and they are well aware of it.

Metal on metal resounds anew. The Emperor aims for the low line this time.

He wants it to be over as fast as possible.

Like a toreador, Campo avoids the blow by spinning around, and while his adversary collapses, lies flat on his back, drooling like a baby, Campo places the tip of his blade on the spot over the heart.

Will he dare?

The man who thinks he is a Caesar, the alpha male with a thousand mistresses, the conqueror of Abyssinia, friend of Churchill's and Hitler's, today, the most beloved man in Italy (and in a few years, surely the most reviled) is at his mercy, ashen-faced with fear, pleading for leniency.

What is it that crosses Antonio's mind at that very instant?

Who, or what, is he thinking about?

About his personal glory? The ghosts of history? Nora and his three daughters, left behind in Turin, who have not seen him in six months? Starace the Terrible? Count Ciano?

The tip of the sword is still pressing against the spot over the heart.

Campo suddenly has a dizzy spell. He staggers back, shuts his eyes, leans against the window.

Outside, it has started to rain again.

Campo will forever remember this moment, in Taormina, during the storm, in the devastated great hall, where the Emperor was at his mercy, the tip of the sword pressing down on the spot above the heart. His eyes showed astonishment. But at the same time a secret irony, something akin to jubilation, a relief, perhaps, that he was dying under the sword of the little photographer who had, for so many long years, in the silence of his laboratories, crafted, almost piously, the image of his idol.

Wasn't it after all in the natural order of things? Is a human god — much too human — not meant to be burned by the very hands of those who have created his glory and who have adored him?

Like his master, Antonio is an obstinate progenitor.

"A girl again!" he predicts with his usual clairvoyance when Nora, a few weeks later, announces a happy event.

It's a boy. Antonio is wild with joy. They call him Paul.

In Turin, it is all about visions. When you come out onto a piazza, you find yourself in front of a stone man who gazes at you as only statues know how to gaze. At times the horizon is limited by a wall behind which are the long drawn out sounds of a locomotive whistling, a train rumbling as it moves off: all the nostalgia for infinity is revealed to us behind the geometric precision of the piazza.

These are unforgettable moments that we are witnessing when certain aspects of the world, whose existence we did not even suspect, suddenly appear and unveil those mysterious things that were already there within our reach, at every moment, without allowing our too short vision to distinguish them, or our too imperfect senses to perceive them.

Their muted calls, arising so close to us, but resonating like voices from another planet, can be but rarely picked up by our human ears, which are only used to the logical noises of life.

Giorgio De Chirico

Swirls of light. Intoxicating vertigo of images, of music, of official lies.

Campo will be the first, on May 9th 1936, at about ten thirty at night, in front of 200,000 people gathered on the Piazza Venezia, to see the mask begin to crack.

Heralded by the sound of trumpets, he steps out on the balcony, chin jutting forward, hands resting on the balcony guardrail, eyes half-closed, and begins to speak softly, giving full reign to the growing emotion in his voice.

"The Italian people have built this empire with their blood. They will make it fertile with their work... Armed with this supreme truth, legionnaires, raise up your banners, your weapons and your hearts! Raise them high and, welcome, after fifteen centuries, the resurrection of the Empire on these fateful hills of Rome. Will you prove worthy?"

The crowds: "Yes! YES!"

The Emperor withdraws.

They call him back to the balcony forty-two times.

Finally, he collapses on a chair, destroyed, and bursts into sobs.

Campo captures a last image, but he shows it to no one: he realizes that this is the end of the film.

VI

On the 13th of May, 1932, Julien is hired by a match factory, The Diamond Company Inc., where twenty men and fifty women are employed as unskilled workers. The factory is located behind the train station, right in the heart of the little town of Nyon.

Even from a distance, you can hardly miss its huge chimney and the hundreds of tree trunks stacked up along the train tracks.

At the Diamond, Julien is responsible for the vats where the kerosene and the paper pulp are melted, as well as for the maintenance of the machinery. As the matches (made of poplar wood) are carried forward on the conveyor belt, the kerosene and the pulp are automatically added. The following machine then stacks the matches in small piles. Female workers then make the drawers face the right way and the small piles fall into the drawers.

Once they are full, the boxes then pass through a machine that coats the striker with glue and pulp and they move on to a drying fan. Finally they go to packaging.

Each woman checks about 72,000 match boxes a day.

In 1932, at the Diamond, Julien earns one hundred francs bi-weekly. He goes to pick up his envelope on Friday nights in the office of the director, a Swede called Mister Widgren who isn't easy to get along with.

He works about ten hours a day.

The first year, he is entitled to one day of vacation.

It is a dangerous job, especially if you don't see very well.

When he fills the machine with the baskets of matches, they rub against the metal plate and catch fire. Every man for himself! He tries to protect himself with his hands, with part of his work smock, but then the smock catches fire!

At the Diamond, this happens every week: the machines are like tubes and turn into flame-throwers. Sometimes there is only one way out: jump out the window to escape from the blaze.

Early one morning, he set off on the road to Duillier. But, for once, he didn't stop in front of the inn with the closed shutters, he continued on his way towards the mountain; he walked briskly once he had passed the Château de Coinsins with its two T-shaped wings and the red Mansard style roof.

After a rainstorm, the road is full of ruts and looks wrinkled like a withered skin. He has to jump between the puddles and be careful not to slip on mossy stones.

Between Genolier and Begnins, there is an oak forest. In its center lies a pond that people call the green lake, but, in this season, it is no more than a muddy bog for its water has almost entirely disappeared

He loves the silence of these woods. He is in total solitude and shadows reign supreme. A place where he is safe from ghosts. He sits down on a tree stump. He empties his flask of white wine. He eats his bread and cheese.

Sometimes in summer, he stumbles over a gray inert mass lying in the middle of the path: it is a viper with a huge stomach, surrounded by the debris of its shedding skin, as it digests the shrew it has just caught and swallowed.

Meanwhile, Emilie stays home. This she doesn't like. She takes her son to school.

She prepares Julien's lunch box. She goes out to tea with her friends. She often dreams of a large cinderblock terrace where a chestnut tree and a plane tree grow, a terrace that dominates the vineyard and the lake.

In the pond behind the game of ninepins, trout and gray carp chase each other, and there, at the foot of the pond, is an old tricycle lying on its side.

Pierre does not like school. But he has no choice.

The instructor doesn't like him either: he is a short man, with a triangular face framed by a stiff gray goatee.

He picks on Pierre who is punished unfairly more often than anyone else, is sent to the corner where he spends entire mornings wearing a dunce cap, is victim of unmerciful teasing by his classmates, and is given lashes after every recess.

There are few images from this period.

Some female workers, in profile, filling baskets with match boxes or coating the strikers with glue and pulp; others assembling the finished packs consisting of ten books of matches before wrapping them up and then expediting them to the four corners of the world.

Not a single photo of Julien at work.

The only image where he is recognizable was taken in May 1934, at the restaurant of the Schilthorn, for the annual social gathering of the personnel. Everyone is posing at the entrance of the Waldrand restaurant. The women are wearing hats and white blouses. The men in dark suits are wearing traditional or bow ties and, on their heads, boater hats. Most of them are holding a bamboo walking stick. All of them are looking at the camera with a serious expression or with an artificial smile.

All of them?

No, not all of them; there is one man, at the top left of the snapshot, leaning against a column, who is staring out into empty space: it is Julien.

In winter at the factory, there is no heat. The cold is bone-chilling for those arriving early in the morning.

There is a pipe that brings the matches down into the machine. Since this pipe gives out strong heat, everyone gathers round to warm up. Then the boss shouts out:

"Let's go, ladies and gents, let's get to work!"

At noon, everyone goes home. There is no cafeteria, not even a little hot water to heat a pan. The women who come from far away eat in the factory. They go down to the lower level near the basin with the hot water where the mass for the matches is melted down. In pairs, one on each side, they extend a string, then they soak their cans in the water to reheat their lunch. Some of them eat at their worktables surrounded by debris from the matches.

Since the turn of the century, the tips of matches have been made of white phosphorous. It is a substance that ignites easily. Accidents often occur.

Once, Julien burned his hand. Another time, his hair caught on fire (this is why, ever since that day, Emilie makes him wear a cap). Still another time, a jet of fire hit him full in the face with such force that it resulted in second-degree burns.

If they had not been protected by the lenses of his glasses, his poor eyes would have melted.

He has been bed-ridden for ten days, suffering like the damned. Emilie has remained at his side, disinfecting the wounds on his face with salves and ointments.

As for his eyes, she applies warm compresses soaked in chamomile every hour.

When they visit, his mates from the Diamond always bring a bottle of Féchy, dry deli sausage, and salted *bricelets*. They sit next to Julien's bed. They unwrap their picnic. They swap the latest stories about the factory. They are happy to see him again.

Often, at the end of the afternoon, they play cards boisterously as they empty glass after glass of Chasselas. They belch lustily. They raise their voices. They sing popular songs until they are hoarse

This particular year, the top hit is a zany song created by Ray Ventura's orchestra.

An old friend from Angoulême
Invited me to his place
His house is from the quinzième (15th)
It's old but it's a nice place
As I admired his pretty things
I asked him for a favor
I need to go do that thing
he said: "it's at the neighbor's!"

Emilie knows what to expect so, sensing the coming storm, she seeks refuge in the kitchen where she can avoid the refrain that they pick up in chorus with a single loud voice that makes the walls shake

It's better than getting scarlet fever
It's better than swallowing rat poison
It's better than sucking moth balls
It's better than showing off on the Alma Bridge

In a way, Julien is lucky — luckier at any rate than the old workers at the Diamond who suffer from phosphorus necrosis. First, the poor souls lose their teeth, one after the other, then the disease eats away at their jaw bone. At this point, they emit such a fetid and unbearable odor that no one has the courage to come near them.

They suffer agonies for a year before they finally die in horrific pain.

Now, Pierre is no longer alone: a little brother was born; they called him Jacques in memory of the other, the small white coffin.

Once again, as when they ran their pub, Emilie is overwhelmed and doesn't know which way to turn. She had set her heart on a girl to chase away Jacqueline's ghost. But in no time, she will come to adore the petit Jacques.

She looks after her children herself, the little one who eats like an ogre and the older one whose only desire is to play soccer.

Of all the seasons, summer is his favorite.

School is out!

The schoolhouse has been emptied to make room for the first harvests. Time to go searching for birds' nests and berries; to be on the lookout for the first cherries; to go swimming at the lake beaches; to play soccer to your heart's content.

June 9, 1938: ears glued to the old crystal radio set, Julien and Pierre were on tenter-hooks till the last minute.

But, until the last minute, Switzerland held her own: she beat Germany, the reigning champion, in a memorable match in Paris during the World Cup. The Swiss won, 4 goals to 2, after a heroic game. The German players, wearing Nazi armbands, left the stadium in defeat, heads low.

Rumor has it that the good Aryan holed up in his Berchtesgaden hideout took to his bed with a case of green envy.

Since they are having difficulties making ends meet, Emilie has started look-ing for work.

Her younger brother, Ernest, who has just opened a lamp and light shop, has hired her. She does manual work in the cellars of Ernest's house, a very nice villa with pink stucco walls; it commands a magnificent view from its terrace that gently slopes all the way down to the lake. She makes lampshades starting from metal frames that are assembled and produced in the adjoining workshop.

It is a task that requires precision, concentration and strong fingers. It is a constant fight with glue, scissors, parchment with edges as sharp as a razor and the nylon thread that slices into your fingers.

Many a time have I dreamt of Emilie as she twists the ribbon around the metal shaft, careful to cover it completely so as not to leave even a glimpse of metal, and then as she fastens the heavy parchment to the frame, and finally as she sews it all together with the very solid nylon thread!

In her life there is nothing but sweat, work, resignation. The gods do not smile down on her. It is all she can do to just get through every day the Lord hath made; Emilie, teeth clenched, hair tied up in a bun, head always held high, for she makes it a point of honor to hold her own.

For her, living is a punishment. A long, silent sacrifice.

Just like her mother before her, Emilie allows herself no pleasure, nor any sense of abandon. Never ever does she allow herself to relax or lose control. Nor to smile, nor to love, nor to show any tenderness that might betray her…Never does she allow anything to distract her from her Duty.

She is a fortress of silence.

Could it be she is paying off a debt? Atoning for a crime she did not commit, such a long time ago, an unmentionable vow, a wild and silent desire that pur-sues her night and day, like a curse?

There are days when he can't resist: he leaves the city at the crack of dawn, his camera slung around his neck. He follows the railroad tracks, passes in front of the wooden shacks, smoke rising in the azure sky; he walks through the tunnel and reaches the deserted intersection.

Which road to take? The East road that takes you down to Prangins, the former residence of Louis Napoleon? The South road that leads you straight to the lake? The Western path that brings you to the flower gardens of la Plantaz?

Not a moment's hesitation: Julien follows his shadow on the white road. It is easy to follow, still damp from the night's dreams, uncompromising and quiet. He knows where it will lead him.

In the distance, with a loud crashing of broken branches, black pine trees collapse, as axes bite into the wood, saws wail like ambulance sirens. Julien plugs up his ears.

Fortunately, the road angles away. The sun turns the gray fields to gold. The vineyards on both sides of the road, then the lovely Frêne spring that supplies the entire region with drinking water.

And there, behind a wild rosebush, the inn of the vanished dreams. The doors and the windows are boarded up. The terrace is strewn with leaves, the pond empty, the ninepins abandoned.

Julien aims his Rollei. He cannot see what he is photographing. Shadows dance on the terrace. Grating music from an old record player lingers in the air. Suddenly he feels faint. He needs to sit down on the low slate wall. He rubs the lenses of his glasses.

What is it Julien is looking for during these long solitary walks?

Forgetfulness?

Not necessarily…

It is more likely that he is searching for an alternate world: its path created with each step would be as wide as the horizon and as inaccessible. A world made of becoming, of waiting, of suffering.

Julien travels across the seasons: winter, when all things are abolished and frozen, like a sign; spring when death explodes, when everything opens up, under the assault of the sun, in order to bloom and resuscitate; summer of pounding blood, of wheat on fire and of welcoming shade; autumn, at last, inventing new colors, agonizing sky, desire in suspense.

When he walks like a vagabond, his Rollei around his neck, he recovers a world: a world of birdsong and light, of perfumes and silence, a world he had never imagined but that he immediately recognizes.

It is only then that he truly can see.

In winter, he sets out blindly, following frozen and muddy paths. His pace is brisk.

The sky is black with snow. He passes the hospital and turns left, towards the village of his childhood.

The grass, burnt by the night frost, crackles under his feet.

Lights in the windows. But Julien does not stop: he no longer knows anyone here and no one knows him. He passes in front of the statue of the ancestors, the courtyard of the farm where once, in the other century, his father split his head with the blow of an axe while he was playing with a ball.

He does not stop there either. He has no regrets, no nostalgia. He walks on.

Before Borex, he turns right. There isn't even a road, just a muddy yellow trail. Winter has chased away the birds. The beech trees are white with frost. The silent forest calls to him.

Zigzagging between the trees and pools of snow, Julien goes all the way down to the stream. The water meanders in places, between the green mossy rocks. Julien gathers a few drops, moistens his lips and sits down. He takes out the camera, aims it at the tree-tops consumed by the light, at the pebbles in the stream, the devastated ferns, the dark pine trees, the frozen pond.

Under the transparent ice, a little girl with blond hair is calling out, her mouth full of dirt, her hands red with cold, her eyes, the color of ashes, stare up at him.

Now it is Julien's turn to cry out. No sound will come out of his mouth.

He turns and runs off as fast as his legs will carry him. He keeps running until he reaches the first village. He huddles in a corner of the café. He orders a hot toddy. He remains there for hours meditating in the vapors of the rum. He tells no one (anyway, who would believe him?).

Julien waits for night to fall, for Emilie or another woman to come fetch him, for someone to finally deliver him from his ghosts.

They are seated in the kitchen. Emilie her nose buried in her pots and pans, Julien, ears glued to the radio, on the alert for the sports bulletin that usually follows the evening news.

This tune is full of joy and melancholy.

When happiness comes your way
You must learn to take advantage of it
When you hold all the trump cards
You must not hesitate
Let us pick all the roses along the way
Why put all off till tomorrow
What are we waiting for to be happy?

Without exchanging a word, they look at each other, and tears run down both their faces.

The same image, at the same moment, emerges from their memory: an enchanted inn amidst the vines, a cinderblock terrace with, on both ends, a game of ninepins on one extremity and a pond replete with carp and trout, at the other, an over-turned rusty child's tricycle.

What are we waiting for to be happy?
What are we waiting for to celebrate?
There are violets
All you could want
There are red grapes, white and blue
Butterflies take off two by two
And the centipede puts on his socks
The Larks flirt with each other
What are we waiting for to be happy?

And over there, by the door, in her light batiste dress, a little girl with turquoise eyes, stares at them sweetly with a look of reproach. Her lips move a little. She looks as if she were speaking. But no one can understand what she is trying to say.

The secret child drowns himself in music. It is his water, his fountain of youth, his internal sea. He is able, at any moment, to revisit the faces and voices of those he has loved. Time doesn't exit. Death is obsolete.

For Julien and his friends, it is a tune by Ray Ventura and his orchestra that they all pick up in chorus. For Emilie, it is a song performed by Jean Nohain and Mireille ("Sleeping in the Hay") that she croons in secret and which takes her back to the enchanted harvests of her childhood, on the great family farm.

As for Antonio, he does not like words to be set to music: Grieg melodies do not need saccharin stories, or mushy poetry to be naturally suave.

For Nora, it is the voice of the great Caruso and whatever words he pronounces do not matter.

Julien has never gone back to work. He has a small disability pension for the burns that remain a memory imprinted on his face. He never removes his cap He spends his days on the terrace, playing cards with his former co-workers from the match factory. He plays Jazz or poker. And since his eyesight is very bad, he has circled all the numbers on the cards with a thick black line to better distinguish them.

His only activity, now, is to take photos: his camera slung over his shoulder, he walks around the town, guided by a voice, a scent, a familiar gesture. The lapping of a fountain. The laugh of a friend from the Diamond. The canvas from a scaffolding flapping under the onslaughts of the wind. The white spots of sail boats. The lake, the color of mercury

What is the use of photography?

To give a face to all that will be lost.

On Sundays, Julien and Emilie take the little red train to Barillette. Pierre carries the picnic basket, Julien, the bottles, and Emilie carries Jacques in her arms.

As soon as they arrive, they pick a quiet spot on the edge of the forest where they will spend the whole day. Julien spreads a big blanket on the grass, in the middle of gentian, crocus and wild daisies. Pierre sets off in search of blueberries, Little Jacques plays with a soccer ball in the pasture.

It is a magical moment: the folds of the mountain almost as far as the eye can see, like ocean dunes. The acid green of the short grass grows darker and deeper within the larch forest. Water troughs carved into tree trunks where water flows, drop by drop, where moss and tadpoles thrive. Pebbled paths disappearing into the woods.

An agonizing silence as if on the threshold of another world.

The secret child has his eyes wide open. He has always recorded everything, sorrow and tears, moments of happiness, faces that frown and those that laugh. Like a wound, his eyes never close.

After touring the wine cellars, then rambling through the town until midnight, they find themselves in Rive, in front of the statue of Master Jacques, a painted statue representing a warrior armed with a sword and holding a banner — no doubt, this was the former police chief.

"Mort aux vaches!"[2] cries Julien, climbing onto the fountain to challenge the leader of the men bearing arms.

Around him yelling, waving their arms about and drinking gin straight from the bottle, his drinking buddies continue to egg him on. The intrepid one undertakes the ascent of the bearded and well-endowed hero. He reaches the top, clings as well he can to the plaster banner and lets out a final cry:

"Long live anarchy!"

Then he loses his balance and tumbles, head first, into the fountain, taking down with him Master Jacques, who breaks into more than thirty pieces.

Julien spends the rest of the night in jail.

He is a wild, isolated child: he likes to walk in the dark, blindfolded, groping to find his way with his hands and arms outstretched like a beggar on a pilgrimage to Compostello. And thus the detested day turns into night. The slightest rustle becomes an augur that must be deciphered.

---

2 Literally, "Death to cows!" This insult comes from the Franco-Prussian War (also known as Franco-German War, the 1870 War [19 July 1870 to 10 May 1871]), in reference to the German "Wache," or sentinel, easily changed to "Vache." Eventually, the term would be used as an insult to anyone wearing a uniform in a position of power.

September 1, 1939: Hitler has just invaded Poland.

Jacqueline would have turned twelve today.

Pierre has always abhorred light, blinding nature, the false treasures that belong to the world of the living. His kingdom is down below, amidst the animals. He is the bloated child with a fresh complexion due to purges, the one that a blind father once threw into the cellar—a child of the catacombs. There he has set up a sort of den for himself; a narrow and fetid den which no one dares enter. Every night, he ruminates escape plans.

At about this time, since he can no longer see much of anything, Julien is offered surgery for his poor eyes

"A new technique!" raves the surgeon. "Revolutionary! You will see!"

Julien doesn't give a damn. Emilie has no opinion on the matter. It is Pierre in the end who will manage to convince everyone.

"You have nothing to lose, papa! If the operation is successful, you will see the world with new eyes!"

But does Julien, in fact, truly want to see the world as it is and not as he imagines it to be?

The operation lasts six hours. The surgeon at first performs a vitrectomy, then he repairs, as best he can, the detached and folded over retina—it is the work of an expert silversmith—the object is to delicately apply the fine, sensitive film to the back of the eye without damaging the optic nerve. Finally, the ocular globe is closed again and in place of the vitreous liquid, a special high density gas that creates pressure on the retina and holds it firmly in place is injected.

When Julien awakens the following day, the surgeon cannot hide his joy.

"The operation was a success! You'll see what you will see!"

They still have to wait a few more days, and then, the dressings are removed... Julien's eye, a lovely ruby color, is not a pretty sight. But they uncork the champagne all the same!

"How do you feel, sir?

"Very well, Doctor. But I cannot see a thing!"

"That's of no importance, since the operation was a success."

"But then, when..."

"It will happen, my dear sir, you will see."

Then in a tone full of reproach:

"Don't be so impatient. You must let nature take its course!"

The following days, a slight glimmer of hope

"I think I can make out a window," Julien says, pointing to the open door. "I think I see the sun..."

"You see, dear sir! What did I tell you?"

But by the next day, the window (or the door) has closed again. Julien is once again plunged into the familiar night. He cannot see the flowers that they bring him, but he is drunk with their perfume.

"It's the gas!" proclaims the surgeon with pride. "We must inject the gas again. After that, you will see, everything will clear up!"

This time, the operation lasts less than an hour. But it doesn't go well. It takes place at the end of the morning: the surgeon is upset and nervous, the nurses weary and overwhelmed, and Julien, who has not been put to sleep, screams with pain when the needle is plunged into his eye.

After the operation, he must remain prone on his side for several days, without moving, to let his damaged retina return to its proper place in the back of the eye and not move...But Julien is tired of listening to the doctor's orders. He drinks and plays cards with his old mates from the Diamond. In the common room, they raise Cain, they sing Charles Trenet songs. They smoke cigars. They pinch the buttocks of the nurses.

When he is kicked out of the hospital, everyone is relieved.

He walks amongst ghosts, on a path that grows darker with each step. No matter! Julien could follow it with his eyes closed. He knows each tree, each house, each field of clover or corn by heart. The large pond with its dead water. The grave-like trenches of beets and cabbage.

Then the church appears, boxed in by two white cherry trees, the tall bell tower covered with tiles.

He pushes the gate open, the air is blistering hot; a perfume of roses and violets welcomes him; the birds cry out, whirling in circles around the little forest of tombs. Julien feels dizzy. Blood pounding in his temples. He puts his hands down on a white gravestone. His eyes meet the eyes of a little girl in an enamel medallion. He sits down on a rock right in front of her. He wipes the lenses of his glasses for the thousandth time.

All roads lead to her.

Past the awning, turn left, follow the graveled lane; then, on the right, the row of tall dark cypresses: it is here, in the little forest of tombs, a white stele with a name, two dates sadly close to each other.

Here that her body is resting. What is left of it.

Where is she now?

Julien has never believed in paradise or in the last judgment, or in that hell where souls are perpetually consumed in flames — not in any of all that religious nonsense. He only knows she is no longer here, Jacqueline: no more does she come throw her arms around his neck, no more does she ride the little tricycle, no more peals of laughter on the terrace. She is not under that stone either.

Nor up there in heaven. Nor anywhere else. He wasn't able to hold on to her.

Who will give the lost world back to me?

That obscure world of hills and snow, of streams, of forests, of those seashores bathed in the light of the rain in the evening, together with the scents of salt and storm, of that blue of exchanged glances, the sky disappearing behind the vineyards, that world filled with stars and promises — that world of before me.

VII

Just as he has witnessed (or even aided, according to some) the Duce's dark, radiant spread of influence, Antonio, as both fascinated and mocking witness, will also be involved in the disaster: illness (never acknowledged), fits of madness (always twisted to his advantage), delusions of imperial grandeur (on behalf of the major Arab rulers, he is given the Sword of Islam, which turns Africa into part of the Empire) — the wild desperate flight towards death.

Another of Antonio's images (dated August 18, 1937) shows the Emperor in Sicily, eye glued to a movie camera lens: he is meticulously checking the machine's range, the light, the setting, while the cameraman, who is watching him in action, stands behind his back.

It is an invaluable photo that reveals the Emperor who is staging himself. It is thus a staging of a staging that Antonio captures on that day. He shows us how the image can be ordered, manipulated and altered, and whose eyes hide behind it.

Totally caught up in his narcissism, the Duce, in this case, did not catch and block an image that clearly betrays his total need for power: not only is he (inside) the image, but also its reverse: the invisible eye of God.

Image: magic.

Almost the same word with jumbled letters.

In Antonio's adopted country, they make collections of images. It makes your head swim in a whirlwind of shapes and colors. People endow them with all kinds of powers to ward off evil: a true white magic.

When the Emperor is bored, and this is happening more and more often, he phones Antonio.

"Campo? Are you free this evening…

Perhaps, Sir.

"It is not a question, Campo, it is an order."

"*Si, Signorsi!*"

"Then, meet me on center court at exactly 18 hours."

He wouldn't want to miss these tennis matches at the Quirinale for the world. Even though he no longer has much time to practice, Antonio is still quite a good player. Indeed, didn't he beat hands down, just two months ago, the former Russian champion, Vladimir Nabokov who was temporarily in Trieste, in two straight sets? And later, in Rome, the Sports Minister himself, in a match replete with ups and downs as the government *in corpore* looked on, and after which the arrogant minister was stripped of his portfolio and sent back without further ado to his native Friuli?

It is a mild and melancholy autumn day. Several players, half-heartedly exchanging balls, occupy the clay courts that are still damp after the morning rain. Two young women are busy playing in the central court where the ground, a beautiful brick color, is the finest, and the surface, the most even.

Of course, as soon as he arrives, flanked by the two watchdogs who are always at his side whenever he ventures out, everyone stops playing. Mutterings abound. He is observed with a combination of fear and fascination. Those with the most courage press their noses against the wire-mesh for they don't want to miss a nano-second of this spectacle. The others remain rooted on the spot, racket in hand, mouths agape, like the people of Pompei just before they were mummified in a rain of black ashes.

This evening, you can tell with a glance that he is having one of his bad days, the Emperor of Italy. Usually, he changes right there, on the court: he does it casually and takes his time for he likes to show off his powerful torso, his lion's neck, his muscled arms. But today he looks solemn. He is wearing a little cotton shirt and black pants. He has American canvas shoes on his feet. He has already removed the cover of his old Dunlop racket.

"Problems, Sir?

"Women, they are killing me, Campo. And Italy is a pain in the ass."

"Take a vacation, Sir."

"Impossible, right now. Great upheavals are brewing in Europe. And Italy has got to be part of it."

"Why is that, Sir?"

"You know them as well as I do, Campo: Italians are vain. And History would never forgive me if I were to stand by and do nothing."

"Forget History, Sir."

"To be sure, Campo. But History does not forget me."

"Shall we play, Sir?"

"Let's play, Campo."

As is his wont, the Emperor starts out by playing hard, running after each and every ball, sliding with great agility on the clay court, shutting his eyes as he swings, hitting the ball with extreme violence. Camped out at the far end of the court, Antonio hits back with nonchalance. He manages to return each ball, apparently effortlessly, but he never attacks, counting on the flexibility of his wrist, taking advantage of his sense of placement and his fencer's ability to side- step.

"I am warm now, says the Duce as he removes his shirt. Let's toss for serve."

Today, just like every other time, it is the Master who serves first. His face is dripping with sweat, he looks focused. Facing him, Campo, hopping up and down in place, taps the soles of his shoes with his racquet to remove the red earth, whistles a little Pergolesi melody under his breath. Nevertheless, when the ball bounces in the court in a small cloud of dust, just a few feet away from him, he doesn't even try to reach the ball, Campo, but walks directly over to the other service box and stands behind it to await the next service.

"Good serve, Sir."

Galvanized, the Duce smiles. Clearly, no matter what his mistresses might claim, he is in great shape. The match won't last long. Campo will never make the grade. He throws the ball into the air, whacks it like a lumberjack, watches his missile cross the court, touch the edge of the net and then explode outside the lines.

"Fault."

Second serve.

Without even pausing for breath, the Emperor fires the next shot. The ball spurts across the net, but this time too high, then it crashes into the clay a few centimeters outside the service box.

"Fault" says Campo soberly.

Wild with rage, the Emperor flings his racquet to the ground, rushes over to the other side of the net to verify the ball's contentious point of impact. No possible doubt: the serve is clearly out. With the handle of his racquet, Campo draws a little circle in the red ground.

Without a word, the Duce returns to his place behind the baseline, and, to Antonio's amazement, prepares to serve again.

"15 all, utters Campo as he returns to his place.

— But I haven't...

"With all due respect, Sir, you have already served twice."

"What of it? The Emperor is entitled to a third serve!"

"No, *Signornò!* In tennis, there is no third chance."

Disconcerted, the Emperor loses ground at each exchange. He wears himself out running back and forth, from one side of the court to the other. He swipes in thin air. He sprays the tarps. He raises clouds of dust. He curses Saint Anthony and Pope Pius XI.

After an hour of play, pate glistening, eyes reddened by sweat, the Emperor collapses on the net. The spectators move on (and melt into the night) filled with joy at having witnessed the lesson their Caesar and Master has just received, but filled with fear as well because of his expression heavy with foreboding.

The following day, after an almost sleepless night, the Emperor reaches a decision: playing tennis will be prohibited on every court in Italy.

By dint of images and speeches, Italy is preparing herself for war. First Ethiopia, that served as a kind of appetizer, then the Spanish War at the sides of Franco that allowed a further whetting of the appetite, but now it is time to get down to business. The masses are whipped into a frenzied desire for combat. Conditions favorable to national mobilization are created. They make use of every available resource to further their clever propaganda

As part of this effort, I imagine that Antonio played a prominent role by disseminating carefully selected images of the Emperor, and by focusing the hatred of the masses on his toughest adversaries.

Here we have an image that must have traveled around the world: it shows Mussolini at the head of a regiment of *bersaglieri* (among these a number of officers with chests bristling with medals) advancing in jogging mode towards the grandstand.

By the way he frames this close-up and his genius for staging, Antonio has managed to illustrate one of the Emperor's favorite themes: the recovery of the nation through the intensive practice of sports.

As always, the Emperor is in front, wearing a general's cap and black leather gloves, blue eyes riveted on the horizon. He is the one who sounds the charge, who sets an example, who shows the Brown Shirts the road to victory.

Nevertheless, there is also a comical aspect to this photo. Whereas the Emperor is smiling, the dignitaries who accompany him can barely repress their anger at being treated like children and all of them are grimacing.

Veni, vidi, scripsi: I came, I saw, I wrote.

Just like his Caesar and Master, Antonio lives in the historical past: he came to see, and then he wrote what he had seen.

In his own particular way, of course, by mastering the play of light, by playing with perspective and optics, by drawing outlines and volumes onto light-sensitive paper by constructing in the secret of his laboratory, day after day, the impeccable statue of the Emperor, who also lives history in the historical past.

However, on his way home in the early morning mist his eye glides over an apple tree in bloom, over busy waiters who are serving the first *moretti* at sidewalk cafes, the historical past within him falls apart. It is erased by what strikes the eye in that instant, the rustling leaves of the trees, the shifting monochrome of the Po that rolls its blue and gray waters, the red sun breaking through the clouds, the invincible continuous present which is Nora's domain and which Antonio, who is too busy sculpting his images, will never know.

Here is a rare image (taken, no doubt, by Nora): Antonio is surrounded by his daughters and his son Paul, on the banks of the Po, in September of 1937, in front of Mont des Capucins.

Hands in his pockets, a faraway look in his eyes, he has the charm of a dandy with no cares, whereas everyone else—even petit Paul who is making a face, even Pierrette and Elvire who are tilting their heads—all are making an effort to look into the camera, Antonio seems detached and is obstinately looking off into the distance, *elsewhere.*

What the eye of the camera sees is a man who walks through life as a dreamer. See how innocent he is! Light. Elsewhere. Elegant. He is bored, he is serious, he is lost, he enjoys himself for a moment. He is full of irony, of wisdom, of sadness. Only his absent-mindedness makes him look human.

In his blind stubbornness, his honesty, his simplicity, his silence, he is the consummate artist.

During this period, the "Master" also has himself photographed in the role of *pater familias*, sometimes with Rachele and their five children, sometimes with one or the other child on a bicycle, sometimes with the youngest, Romano, perched on the neck of his horse and sometimes in aviator gear framed by his two older sons, Vittorio and Bruno.

When his strength starts to wane, he likes to be portrayed as an exceptional genitor, a man who casts his seed to the four winds, a patriarch with an endless supply of semen.

As long as he lives, Campo will never forget those sessions interspersed with arguments, with screams and threats, the official family arriving that very same morning from Milan to a palazzo still perfumed with the lingering scents of La Dalser or La Petacci (who are never very far removed.)

The dirty skies of Turin.

Long gone now, the images of the bare-chested, half-god threshing the wheat in the midst of Romagna peasant girls, or running bare-foot and bare-chested on the beach of Riccione!

Now, the Master remains locked-up for days on end, sometimes weeks, in his apartments. No one is allowed to see him. He buries himself in silence. He even refuses to see his mistresses, who leave, outraged and furious, after hours of waiting in vain (la Petacci, in a fit of anger, has even set fire to the living-room, using an old love letter).

What a sad sight is the Master when he leaves his home, hands on his stomach, grimacing with pain. His step is unsteady. His speech, once so voluble is jerky, self-conscious, barely comprehensible.

Even his laugh rings out false.

Antonio is there on January 9, 1938, when the Master grants a private audience to Georges Oltramare, the head of the National Union who has come from Geneva to convey greetings on behalf of the Swiss militants.

He is a smooth-talker with a loud voice who pronounces sharp sentences that sound memorized. He has appeared in a few French B movies and seems to be always at the ready for cinema lights.

When the Duce informs him of his reluctance to deal with anti-Semitism, Oltramare blusters:

"It's not a matter of eating or not eating the Jew: what is essential is being able to vomit him out."

In spite of his disgust, the Duce has gone to the trouble of autographing a photo for him.

In the days that follow this exchange, overcome by a wave of nostalgia, he talks to Antonio about Switzerland where he worked for a wine-merchant, then as a packer in a warehouse, a butcher-boy, a policeman and had a thousand other jobs as well. He admires this country without a history, this country that granted him asylum when he had left Italy to avoid military service.

"It was a period when I would sleep under the stars, under Lausanne bridges!"

He tells him about a small village located exactly half-way between Geneva and Lausanne.

"It was at Nyon, in the years 1904 and 1905, I was attending a political meeting in a small overheated room, where labor union activists came from all over Europe in order to participate. In a dark corner was a man with a goatee, wearing a black cap, taking notes. It was Lenin himself! His eyes had an extraordinary intensity! I've never seen him again."

In the eyes of the photographer, Switzerland epitomizes the age of *princeps*[3]: the age of the first images. We can see the Master (who is still a nobody), wearing a close-fitting coat and wing collar, a small, manicured mustache, with the thoughtful look of a conscientious student.

These images are not Campo's, but he will keep them for a long time in his archives, as original proofs for all his future images.

In May 1938, Hitler comes to Italy along with his cohort of collaborators.

On the platform of the Rome Station, Campo is there, of course, in the first row of photographers.

He finds the little man disgusting, strapped too tightly in his parade uniform. To look less pale, he has put rouge on his cheeks. When he speaks or when he walks around his mannerisms are those of a young maiden. He looks like a drug addict who can't come out of his drug- induced trance.

At night, he wakes up the whole Quirinal as he walks the halls half-naked, a candle in hand, screaming:

"I want a man!"

The war is about to begin, for sure now. The Englishman Chamberlain and the Frenchman Daladier — these ingenious and dangerous men — are the only ones left who can pretend to ignore it.

The Emperor has his people well under control. The opposition is decimated. Enemies have been reduced to silence. The desire to come to blows rises little by little among the population.

Livia loves empty churches, their silence, the scent of altar candles and incense.

In Turin, she likes to meditate at the church of la Grande-Mère-de-Dieu, on the other side of the Po, with its immense dome and its fake Roman pillars. Just as she loves reading, she loves praying, this silent dialogue between two solitudes. At times she combines both pleasures: she sits in a small chapel, at a remove from the children and the ostentatious church-goers; she takes a book out of her bag and begins to read Manzoni's poetry or Boccaccio's tales by the soft light of the altar candles.

---

3 The first in time or order, foremost

These are rare moments in which the sacred joins silence and solitude. She feels the increased throbbing of the blood coursing through her veins. She breathes faster and faster. Silent voices resonate in her bosom. It is an ineffable and deep ecstasy that pervades every instant.

It is only then that Livia arrives at the heart of the secret.

It is the eve of war: Hitler is preparing to invade Austria.

In Italy, they have never trusted the Germans and they don't have much affinity for those military displays, those incendiary speeches, this desire for power by which the Nazis are driven. For Italy has never had designs on her neighbors and the only war of expansion that she has waged in Africa ended up in a fiasco.

Therefore they distrust these highly publicized meetings between the two heads of State.

It will be up to a Jew [4], a few years later, to show better than anyone else all this ridiculous pomp in the famous scene from the *Dictator*: both men are shown in barber chairs, each one fighting to be higher than the other and both end up falling on their butts on the floor.

Little by little, the meetings become less frequent: the man who had once been the most photographed in the world (and therefore the most despised and the most worshiped) will from now on be holed up in his den.

Running out of images, Campo has no other option but to recycle old photos, which he resets and touches up as best he can. Without quite falling into disgrace, he lets the salons, the secret reunions, the diplomatic trips disappear little by little from his life. He is no longer in demand. His images still get published in Italy, France, England, Switzerland, but they no longer elicit a response.

Like a long lost friend, Campo reencounters Turin, his second homeland. It is a hardworking and stubborn city, but at the same time, nonchalant and prone to daydreaming.

---

4 Chaplin was not Jewish, but was placed on Hitler's list as a Jew who was to be exterminated. Google Nazi propaganda book reveals Charlie Chaplin was on Hitler's death list. Charlie Chaplin Jew. As the Little Tramp, he made millions laugh. But the Nazis never saw the funny side when it came to Charlie Chaplin. Adolf Hitler's hatred of the politically outspoken movie star is apparent in a yellowing book of Nazi propaganda which includes Chaplin in a hit list of prominent Jews. *http://www.dailymail.co.uk/news/article-520648/Nazi-propaganda-book- reveals-Charlie-Chaplin-Hitlers-death-list.html*.

Antonio discovers it with a brand new eye, just as he rediscovers his family: Livia who is almost sixteen years old, has long brown braids that frame a face with a surly look; Pierette is fourteen; Elvire almost twelve; and petit Paul is fast approaching six.

He has traveled all through Italy for such a long time in his quest for images, thousands of negatives, constructing a veritable profane mythology one piece at a time — and he has seen nothing of what was happening right there, in front of his eyes, in his own family.

VIII

It is like a bad dream: first there was Munich, handshakes, smiles for the cameras, cheers of victory, sighs of relief. Then the pact between Stalin and Hitler. Then, following a long period of intimidation, the invasion of Poland. And suddenly, as if ignited by a single match, all of Europe was set ablaze!

In Switzerland as well, men of fighting age are being mobilized. Monitoring of the borders is reinforced. Goods are rationed. Plans for resistance are being elaborated. There is a state of permanent alert.

Julien has passed the age of serving (besides, he wouldn't be much of a soldier as he might score against his army buddies rather than against the enemies of the mother country). Pierre is too young to sign up for the army. Jacques has just turned seven.

A bloodbath is about to begin. They will not be part of it.

Every morning, Pierre reads the headlines to Julien and gives him a detailed description of the images of Pétain, Hitler, or Mussolini, noting how they are always frozen in triumphant postures.

Julien can't manage to put a face to these names.

When the English planes are on their way to bomb Milan or Turin, they always pass above the town around midnight. People come out on their terraces, wave at them; they have small blue and red lights.

And Pierre, rejoicing in the night, gives them his blessing:

"Come on, let's go, guys! Knock the living hell out of them!"

But, when they are on their way back, four hours later, the same people feel a pang of anguish, they know homes have been destroyed, bridges demolished, villages in ruins, and families are counting their dead. Now they are quiet.

The press — like the official radio broadcasts — must be very cunning to escape the wrath of the military censorship that was established from the very beginning of the war so that every event might be given an acceptable interpretation.

Most of the images are meant to be edifying or dramatic: soldiers taking the oath at the border; young women joining the army or the communication services; peasant women who have come to boost the morale by offering bread and cheese to the young recruits. The other images are carefully handpicked and often touched up: Mussolini, chin jutting forward, but a smile on his lips, is made to appear almost likable: Goering has the ruddy complexion of a bonvivant; Maréchal Pétain has the looks of a debonaire and wise patriarch.

They live History as spectators: it is a nightmare that only catches up with them two or three days, or a week, or perhaps even a month later. No live images, no reporters from the front. Instead, articles based on agency dispatches. Altered photographs. Unverifiable accounts. They live the war through the old crystal radio set in the living room.

They often don't believe what they hear: Belgium has capitulated. German troops have invaded France (how is that possible?). There are air battles in the Jura mountains between the Luftwaffe and Swiss aircraft. The Reich protests. Switzerland apologizes. Hitler pushes the British back to the sea at Dunkerque. In just ten days, humiliated and beaten, France is reduced to silence.

The radio broadcasts German songs, military marches, propaganda speeches.

Have they heard *The Maréchal's* speech in this sinister month of June 1940?

"Since the 1918 victory, the pursuit of happiness and pleasure has trumped the spirit of self-sacrifice. People have felt more entitled to take than they were willing to serve. They looked for shortcuts, unwilling to put in the effort. And today we are facing the disastrous consequences."

Did anyone notice that he was using the exact same words as Pilet-Golaz?

"The Federal Counsel has promised you the truth. It will offer it to you without embellishments and without fear. The time has come for our interior renaissance. Each one of us must shed our old self. This means: no more endless discussions, just conception; no more holding forth, just action; no more enjoyment, just production; no more asking, just giving."

On a Sunday in July, they take the train to la Dôle, walk deep into the forest, stop in a clearing for their picnic.

After the meal, Emilie and Julien take a nap. Pierre and Jacques leave them to go look for mushrooms. They walk along the stream. They climb over little stone walls. They weave through trees and barbed wire fences.

Suddenly, they come face to face with a man armed with a machine-gun. He is wearing a German helmet, an armband with a swastika. He yells out some words at them. Pierre and Jacques make off as fast as they can. The soldier runs after them for a few meters, shouting angrily, branches snapping under his boots; then he bursts into laughter.

Often on autumn mornings, his feet carry him away from the town. He goes through Bois- Bougy, and then climbs towards Crans. The sky is clear. He leaves the main road, takes one of its branches and is soon swallowed up in the thickets.

Then it comes into sight: an erratic bloc twenty-three meters long, ten wide, and six high, that is called the Féline Rock, perhaps in memory of its former owner, Isaac Féline, jam maker in Languedoc, then burgher of the city of Geneva in 1705.

This rock comes from afar: pulled up from an area by the Pissevache cascade in the Valais, it was transported all the way to Crans by the Rhône glacier thousands of years ago.

He scales the rock to the best of his ability, installs himself at the top, takes out the tools from his tool-pouch and gets to work. For months he has been coming here in secret, as if on a pilgrimage. No one knows anything about it: neither Emilie, nor Pierre (who will come to this place several times on school outings), nor, of course, Jacques. He gets to work, patiently, meticulously. He is engraving in the siliceous stone two large intertwined letters, making a kind of secret monogram.

JO

He pours all his heart and courage into it as if these two letters so finely chiseled in the stone, summed up his entire life (the secret of his life).

Noon comes and goes. Julien's thoughts are not turned to food. Gray patches are beginning to take over the sky. Rain suddenly illuminates the forest. Julien, lost in his work, has not even noticed.

The storm now begins its rumblings. Long flashes of lightning slice into the wheat fields. Julien whistles under his breath as he taps on his chisel.

Time after time, nightfall catches him unawares, perched high up on his belvedere. He makes his descent in the dark, hesitantly feeling his way, stumbles, loses his balance, and ends up on all fours in the grass; a stream of curses and he gets back up, adjusts his glasses.

A little bell chimes on the path ahead. Julien calls out.

As in a dream, a harnessed team of two horses with long black manes looms up. The moon is high in the sky, the night filled with ghosts.

Seated in the back of the cart, Julien is still whistling.

It is the end of the year. Butter, tea, milk, and cocoa are rationed. Like everyone else, Julien and Emilie have been ordered to extinguish all the lights in the house as soon as night falls.

Together with his brother, Pierre spends his time in the cellars. He plays soccer on the gravel, in those corridors smelling of urine and dampness, of fruit drying on the shelves and of cheap wine. He plays by candlelight.

For four years, Pierre writes to a soldier he doesn't know, but who is his *war god-father.* He is a remarkable man, exceptionally well read, and a rare etymology buff. He is garrisoned somewhere in the Jura. His name is Jacques Adout.

Meat, coffee, and bread are rationed now.

Four mouths to feed in these times of famine is a lot to ask. Especially when there is no money. So, without giving him a choice, they send Pierre to German Switzerland, near Davos, to an elderly *boulanger* (baker) who has placed an ad in the classified section of *Le Journal de Nyon* because he was looking for an apprentice.

There, at the other end of the world, Pierre is provided with room and board, clothes cleaned against the whitewashed walls. He is up at three in the morning to help the boss and to take the bread out of the bakery ovens. Then, he has to go deliver the goods with a rickety sleigh that he must maneuver as best he can along the snowy paths.

When he returns, he is so exhausted that he dozes on and off till the evening.

But his day is far from over: he has to help the baker knead the dough, then prepare the oven, go and fetch the wood, light and keep feeding the fire to ensure that it remain constantly at the same temperature.

And it all starts over again just a few hours later, with the deliveries as he struggles against great gusts of cold wind.

Every evening for the next three years, his grub will consist of dried prune tart.

On the walls of the town, a single slogan:
"HE WHO CANNOT BE SILENT DOES HARM TO HIS COUNTRY."

In Davos, he is completely cut off. He has no newspapers (except for the soccer articles that Emilie cuts out and sends to him once a month). He doesn't listen to the radio. He has no friends, no acquaintances. He is in total ignorance of the Japanese attack on Pearl Harbor and he never hears the speech delivered by von Steiger, the Federal Counselor, stating that in Switzerland *the boat is full* and there is no more room for refugees. He never hears of the German capitulation at Stalingrad nor of the fall of Mussolini.

In his lost valley, he is so miserable that he writes every day to his parents: the boss is a monster. He makes him work like a slave. He is violent and quick-tempered. He always keeps a bottle of kirsch or prune liqueur within reach. His own children despise him.

Should Pierre be late coming back from his deliveries, the old man releases his own pent-up rage by dint of lashes with a whip.

His childhood: a mass grave where black crows, broken toys, a little music box whose distended and rusty spring creaks out a rosary of tinny sounds are all gathered in a jumble.

The secret child never sees the light of day. Like a pending letter, he is just there in a corner of a cupboard or of a cellar, or deep in the catacombs. He is passed from hand to hand without a look, a word of parting or of tenderness. But the sealed message travels through time. The wax develops tiny cracks. The paper becomes transparent. The words written in red ink begin to fade like a very ancient drawing.

He remains seated for hours on end, almost prostrate, in the doorway, listening to the noises of the world, the accents of this language with sounds like rolling gravel, gazing at the heavy sky above his head which is beginning to open ever so slowly on a more distant sky, a sky of the purest blue, only able to exist in the hope that someone is going to come, one day soon, perhaps tomorrow, that something is about to happen in this world.

This image is one that will remain in her eyes for a long time: the Saphis cavalry galloping on white horses in the snow, two by two, in impeccable order, amongst the cries of the children and ululations of the furious riders!

Defeated without ever going into battle, displaced in a war for which they were not prepared, they are now gathered in Swiss meadows, reluctant prisoners, for an ultimate (and derisory) fantasia. Some come to drink the fountain waters; others march through the villages in full parade attire, foreheads adorned with little bells; others stand guard in front of the customs bunkers.

Emilie has never seen anything like it: horsemen wearing djellabas and red turbans, rifles slung across their shoulders, and only simple leather sandals on their feet! She thinks they cut a handsome figure, in their bruised pride and their provocative appearance...

He loves, when the morning is still young, to go down to the lake. In winter, the harbor is deserted. The boats, covered in green tarp, rock gently while the (bitter) North wind whistles through the masts. Seagulls fighting over a few breadcrumbs on the dock. Snow sparkling between the rocks.

The lake is frozen in spots, transparent ice the color of algae and salt. He sits down on a bench between a flaking plane tree and a thorn bush. He packs his pipe in silence. He gazes out at the lake. He is waiting for a boat that will not come.

At last, Pierre has come back home from his private hell: or rather he ran away in the middle of the night from the Davos bakery *(boulangerie)* after an ultimate whipping by a master who was beside himself with rage because Pierre, just to get even, had pissed into the very trough where the old man would knead his dough.

When he reached home, he had spent his last dime, his tattered and torn clothes were filthy, his body covered with bruises.

The blows given, the blows received, the child submits to them and grits his teeth. They remain etched in his memory. Ready to resurface at the slightest provocation. They will return ten, twenty, thirty years later, but in a different form, administered by another hand.

It is a child offered up on an altar, beaten bloody or threatened by the executioner's axe.

As time goes by, the sacrifice is repeated according to a scenario that is never the same, nor ever totally different; it always takes a little blood to appease the wrath of the fathers.

In the evening, gathered around the old crystal radio set, they listen to Sottens, Radio Paris or Radio Toulouse, Beromünster. For a few hours, blood stops running, the cannons are silenced, they believe a new dawn has come, with no more pain and no more tears.

At nine o'clock on the dot, every night, like a call to rallying, they broadcast *La Complainte du Partisan* (The Partisan's Complaint), written in London in 1943 by Emmanuel d'Astier and Anna Marly.

Les Allemands étaient chez moi
On m'a dit résigne-toi
Mais je n'ai pas pu
Et j'ai repris mon arme.

J'ai changé cent fois de nom
J'ai perdu femme et enfants
Mais j'ai tant d'amis
Et j'ai la France entière.

Un vieil homme dans un grenier
Pour la nuit nous a cachés
Les Allemands l'ont pris
Il est mort sans surprise.

Le vent souffle sur les tombes
La liberté reviendra
On nous oubliera
Nous rentrerons dans l'ombre.

When they poured across the border
I was cautioned to surrender
This I could not do
I took my gun and vanished.

I have changed my name so often
I've lost my wife and children
But I have many friends
And I have all of France.

An old man in a garret
For the night did he hide us
The Germans came and took him
He died with no surprise.

The wind blows across the graves
Freedom will come again
We will be forgotten
We will disappear in the shadows.

As he sings along with the *"Complainte du Partisan,"* a strange idea takes shape in Pierre's mind: music is stronger than any dictatorship.

Thirty years later, this heart-rending song will be revived by a singer with a deep voice and a morose disposition, a Canadian from Montreal by the name of Leonard Cohen and will be a hit that will be broadcast on every radio station. It will be one of the first songs he will learn to play on the guitar, the secret child; and he will perform it in summer at those family reunions where all the relatives are assembled in full force either at the Lucca house or at the Lido di Savio on the Adriatic Coast, but he will never understand that particular look of astonishment that will then appear on the faces and in the eyes of those he loves.

Silence has always been their daily bread.

It is the custom in Switzerland, in old Protestant families. It goes hand in hand with humility, respect for the Law, the value of money and frugality (whence the emergence, at the same time as the Reformation of *secret bank accounts*) Never speak at the table, nor in school, nor at church: nothing personal must ever transpire or be given a voice. Moments of doubt or deep emotions, hatred that lasts a day or for just ten minutes: all of this simply does not *take place*.

Julien is now privy to every secret the villages of the Coast have ever held.

Dully, Bursinel, Rolle, Perroy, Promenthoux: these are names that sing in his mind like a familiar refrain. He has walked their streets, explored them, loved them down to the smallest stone. More often than not alone, but sometimes together with petit Pierre, who is always curious to learn about everything, always on the lookout for birds, a fox caught by surprise near an embankment, a stray dog, head hanging low.

He knows them by heart, these villages with red roofs, quiet beaches, fishing boats gently rocked by the currents. Nevertheless, at nightfall, he can't find his way back. He is left stranded on the beach. Julien can't remember where he is, or who he is. Pierre is the one, then, who brings him home, in tatters, hair disheveled, chin gray with stubble.

Pierre is his scout, his faithful, taciturn guide.

Oh those small escapades! How Julien wishes he didn't have to come back!

What is it he is trying to escape?

What crime, what fault needs atonement?

As he walks alone over hills and through the woods, he is seeking that legendary country, the one he beholds at night with his eagle eyes, the forgotten country filled with music and silence, with children's cries, with unbelievable colors, with perfumes of harvested hay, of blackberries, and of red apples.

Julien: indefatigable legs, eyes turned inwards.

With amazing dexterity, Emilie winds her ribbon around the metal shaft, and then, with a very strong thread, she sews the parchment to the frame of the lamp. She repeats this process a hundred times a day. This is her job, her silent destiny, like the lacemaker modestly bent over her work. She has developed calluses on her fingertips, like corns. There are days when she is in pain, an agonizing pain, but she doesn't complain. She works in silence in a kind of cellar together with the other women, and inhales air thick with glue and turpentine vapors that make her dizzy.

Emilie: she of the industrious magic fingers in constant motion.

At night, Julien drinks, getting happy by himself at his table, hallucinating in silence. His eyes light up. His gloomy thoughts run unbridled. He sinks into a dark hole with a dry white wine from the Coast and in this darkness he tries to catch sight of something. The alcohol opens his eyes but at the same time it weighs his body down with an immense weight — at least a ton of flesh like lead.

Yes, his mind becomes sharper and his tongue looser. On the paths that are at last clear, he scrutinizes the night and its ghosts. He strains to hear. He questions. He says nothing.

Faces partially erased by the rain. A fox caught by surprise at the edge of a cliff. Smothered cries of children. Burning stacks of hay or autumn leaves, smoke wafting in the night.

Throughout his bouts of delirium heavy with marc grappa and gentian liqueur, nothing is ever revealed. Only flashes of lightning followed by visions that are so vivid and so violent that his pupils are on fire. Julien can't recall anything about what continues to consume him, but he calls out, and sometimes, when the liqueur is of a high quality, when the night is favorable, a voice answers him. It is always the same voice, muffled by the sound of crashing waves.

A little girl in a white dress whose thin high-pitched voice sounds like mermaids softly calling.

It goes without saying that Julien has never seen the sea, nor the ocean—and he will never see them. He doesn't believe in mermaids either. He has never read Homer or Hans Christian Andersen. He does, however, love to delve into the night that sings the glory of wine. He loves to drown in his glass. He loves to speak with angels in the dark.

Emilie doesn't smoke. Emilie doesn't drink — or if she does, it is in secret, a couple of sips of Port when she is alone in her kitchen. She never lets herself relax. She never lets go of her self-control. Every instant of her life is a continuous struggle. And victory, at the end, only comes at the cost of a sacrifice.

Nevertheless, she likes to dance and party, seek out country dances, going to the circus, playing cards till the wee hours of the morning. But most of all, she likes to make *malakofffs* or *bricelets* for large noisy tables where glasses are generously raised and where demands for food are punctuated by the pounding of knives on the tables.

But the time for that is long gone.

She has no idea how to just be herself, or laze about on sleepy mornings, or even just go for a stroll along the lake. She has always had a gimpy leg but it doesn't prevent her from scurrying to and fro, like a little mouse, for hours on end, back and forth, from the Station to Rive, from the Terrace to Bois-Bougy. She carries enormous lamp shades in her arms, wears an opera hat on her head and black buckle shoes on her feet.

Hobbling along as fast as she can, she cuts through the icy north wind. She is bent over double, her left hand crushing her hat to her head to keep it from flying off. Each step requires a superhuman effort, but she can't be stopped.

Pleasure is intimate and secret, like truth, tears and prayer.

Its cries are smothered. It is not something you can see or mention; in the eyes of others it simply does not exist. It feeds on shadows. It is most often nameless and faceless. It is unmentionable, though not always shameful, dark or forbidden (it is simply denied the right to speak). And yet, it is what constitutes the central core — the living and hidden shadow — of our lives.

When our heart swells with a fervent desire, it is always in secret.

Livia's secret is entering a deserted and fragrant church at dusk to read a Manzoni or a Pavese novel. Julien's secret is walking along country roads as soon as dawn breaks, and taking photos of meadows, horses, water-lilies, clouds in the sky, faces of men and women at work that he will never see. Emilie's secret is being surrounded by her children, her family, friends she might perhaps never see again, but for whom she will prepare the most sumptuous feasts. Antonio's secret, is the music playing in his head and that no one will ever hear for it belongs to him alone and it has no counterpart in the real world. Nora's secret is her silence about her secrets.

"Pierre is a good-for-nothing."

At least that is what his parents think.

School is not for him and every tradesman where he is apprenticed pronounces similar reproaches: obstinate, taciturn, touchy, quarrelsome—and always at a remove from the others, never joining in.

On many an occasion, Julien has taken out on him his own blind fury.

His favorite pastime when he isn't working (and Lord knows he doesn't work very often) is to go to the bowling club near the railroad tracks. Julien knows everyone. These are old buddies, the same gang of fans. He sits on a bench along the sandy playing field and watches the bowlers point or shoot, according to their skills.

Here they play *boules à la lyonnaise,* with large metal *boules* that are buffed assiduously with an old rag before throwing them. Since the boules are shiny and larger than *pétanque boules,* Julien is able to follow them from beginning to end of their trajectory without missing an iota of the spectacle.

One fine day, Pierre decided to leave his master and absconded with all the cash from the workshop till; then, he took the train, the first one on the track, the one leaving for the North and succumbed to the exhilaration of the speeding train.

They catch up with him the following day in Bâle as he is trying to cross into Germany. He gets nabbed so stupidly. He has no passport, but does have a large sum of money in his pockets as well as hidden under his shirt, which immediately makes him look suspicious. He doesn't speak German. He refuses to tell where he is headed. He is very agitated.

That very evening, in handcuffs, trousers torn, framed by two cops like a dangerous criminal, he is released to his parents at the Nyon train station.

Still, Pierre did not desist: he made multiple attempts at running away, breaking out, committing robberies, but every time he got caught.

When they bring him back, however, he is never quite the same. His ears buzz, and in his eyes, a strange unfocused burning light that terrifies anyone he comes across in the street.

Every night, Pierre's head explodes: he is being hunted down in the woods, a horrible din of screams, of wolves baying, of hounds in hot pursuit, running away, running and gasping for breath in the mountain.

Pierre awakens with a start, breathing hard, bathed in sweat.

Day has not yet broken. His pillow is soiled with blood.

It is a ghost, a bundle of anguish and silence, a bundle of scorched photos that gets passed on furtively, under your coat, like a disgusting secret, from father to daughter, from mother to son.

His secret is the night. This is what he experiences every day when he opens his eyes, draws the curtains, turns on the night light in his room: the night is there all around him, oppressive though as light as a fog oozing through the walls.

The night is his light, the air he breathes, his horizon. He has known for a long time that he will never come out of it.

Night and day, Pierre has increasingly violent breakdowns. He dreams of sacrifices, of a bird whose throat is being cut, of a child who is being strangled in his bed. No one is able to console him.

What with the screams of Julien who is sinking into darkness and the breakdowns of her son, it is more than Emilie can endure.

She who used to be in total control of every corner of her kingdom, has stopped scrubbing and polishing her copper pots and pans; she leaves piles of dirty clothes here and there all over the house, no longer goes to church, no longer catches her fingers on the frames of lampshades. Still in her bathrobe, she doesn't bother to get dressed and her days drag by filled with languor and hate. Her eyes are as dark as burnt wine. She has fits of anger over trifles, is always bitter and never stops grumbling.

Her neighbors have nicknamed her the *gendarme*.

Today, father and son came to blows: over a spilled glass, Julien pounded the table with his clenched fist. Pierre answered back with a curse and his father, his face scarlet with rage, abruptly stood up. He tried to grab him by his shirt, but Pierre took a step backwards. And Julien, struggling with a shadow, collapsed first on the table, and then, heavily, on the rug, carrying dishes, cutlery, and bottle of Gamay along with him as he fell making enough noise to wake the dead.

Stunned, he remained seated on the floor for a few seconds, his magnifying lenses on his nose, then anger took over once more. Julien used the dresser to hoist himself back up and threw himself headlong at Pierre. The two men grabbed each other. Julien's lenses flew up into the air. Pierre punched his father in the stomach, in the jaw. He wanted to extricate himself before it was too late, but the blind man is solid. He is steady on his legs and keeps hanging on to his son.

They waltzed around for a few minutes in the living-room, like a drunken couple, despite Emilie's piercing cries from near a window where she had found refuge and where she stood screaming and holding her head in her hands.

Finally, Pierre freed himself. He took a step backwards. Grabbed a chair near the table. He brought it down on the table with all his might. The chair flew into pieces and Julien fell softly on the rug, as if in an American movie, but this time, for real.

At 6pm, in front of the crowd amassed on Piazza Venezia, the Emperor, wearing his full uniform of honorary corporal of the Militia makes the announcement that Italy has entered the war.

"Our goal is to break the chains that keep us asphyxiated within our sea because a country of 45 million inhabitants is only truly free if it has free access to the ocean…"

The theatrics remain the same: from his balcony, the Master exhorts the crowds to follow him, rolls his eyes, raises his voice, looks daggers at all of Italy's enemies. His voice is amplified by loudspeakers and echoes throughout the entire city. Flashes from cameras crackle all around him.

However, despite hysterical calls to murder, Italians don't have the heart for war. No one can see any reason to fight. No one aspires to this ocean that has become, with every passing month, a veritable obsession for the Duce. Perhaps the only way to stay in power and to hide, for an indeterminate time, from Italy as well as the world, the extent of his own ruin.

War-time industries and armories are working full blast. Since the men have left for the front, women and children old enough to work have been recruited. The entire country is running out of steam in its undertaking of this absurd war.

Now bread is being rationed (200g per family, per day) as well as other staples.

With her ration tickets, Nora buys sugar (500 grams per month) and potatoes (3kg per month). Meat is rare and parsimoniously allocated (400g per family and per month).

Once in a while, Campo brings home a pheasant or a hare when he goes hunting. On those days, what a feast: a bowl of *minestra* as appetizer, salad and meat, and an orange from Sicily for dessert.

Poorly prepared, the Italian army equipped with guns dating back to 1891 and with canons taken from Austria after World War I, encounters only reversals. The air force lacks modern aircraft and most of all pilots. In bad shape in Greece, Yugoslavia, Libya, and France, the Italian troops would have been pulverized had the German army not rushed to their rescue.

For all concerned, the cost of war takes too high of a toll. Antonio who has already lost the First World War as an Austrian is about to lose the Second one.

Children who are actually quite alive, but who might perhaps be dead any day soon, Antonio takes photos of hundreds of them that year: these comprise the youth of the fascist avant guard, sons of the she-wolf stamped with the wheat bundle emblem, who are learning how to handle arms in the military camps of Treviso or Rome.

Wearing a strange felt hat decorated with a black braid, they all stand at attention, rifle with bayonet in their right hand, eyes of steel, and white cord espadrilles on their feet.

An officer, wearing a navy uniform, passes them in revue from behind in order to adjust any mistakes in the stance of these young recruits (the eldest is not even fifteen) who are about to be sent off to the great butchery.

Death has arrived; it is continually prowling the streets of Turin. No one has seen it coming (especially not Antonio blinded by the flashes of his camera and his images of glory), but henceforth it will be here, like a shower of stars. A deluge of fire that every night crashes down on the old city.

In a mad dash, they rush down into the cellars. This lasts throughout the entire night: horrifying explosions like earthquakes, smells of gas and smoke, fires that start up in every corner of the city. Nora shivers like all the inhabitants of this improvised shelter, and like Livia, next to her, who listens and watches, but is quiet.

On some nights, in an attempt to overcome her fear, Lydia softly sings a song she has heard on the radio. In the darkness of the cellar, they all hold their breath. The voice of the little girl makes them forget about the exploding bombs.

When they come back up out of their hole, the scene that meets their eyes is unrecognizable: some houses are completely destroyed, others are still exhaling dirty smoke, the others are caved in, there are dead bodies everywhere.

When they came up out of the cellar, an odor of volcano permeated the night air. The storm had washed out the streets. In the distance, in the wake of the bombers, the sky still burned with bursts of fire.

They were so happy, all three of them, so joyous at still being alive in the middle of the rubble that they started to sing against the thunder that resounded in the distance, those great fireworks that lighted up the city.

When daylight is painted blue, when birds sing in the ruins as they had forgotten to do for a long time, when in the morning, women, half blinded by the light, come out of the catacombs, when harmony reigns everywhere in the center of town all the way to Superga hill, then, it is not unusual to hear far off the muffled roar of an exploding mine followed by heartrending screams, inextricably mingled and then an awful silence, almost unreal, and suddenly the sky turns red.

It is a debacle: in May 1943, Italy capitulates to Tunis, then the Allies land in Sicily where they are welcomed as liberators. When he sees these images, Campo rubs his eyes: has he been deluded from the very beginning?

Or did he delude himself? In Lombardy and Piedmont, a wave of strikes assembles over 300,000 workers who demand the Duce's resignation and an immediate exit from the war.

In his apartment on Via Groscavallo, Campo has a ringside seat for taking photos of the banners and fists raised at the sky.

On July 25th, Campo is not in Rome when Mussolini shows up for the royal audience. He is astounded to learn that the little king whom he has always held in contempt, has replaced him as head of the government!

As he leaves the royal villa, he is arrested, carried off, and put into solitary confinement. No one among the ministers and officials of the party makes the slightest attempt to obtain his release.

On the photo, his face is gray, ravaged by fear, eyes dull, mouth twisted in a grimace of stupor.

The following day, Antonio tries to get in touch with the prisoner. It is a lost cause. In solitary confinement, locked up in the penal colony of the Island of

Ponia, the prisoner is surprised to find those political opponents that he had attempted in vain to have assassinated a few years earlier.

During the day, he reads *The Life of Jesus* and at night, since he is unable to fall asleep, he translates into German the *Odes* of the poet Carducci.

On July 29, for his birthday, Antonio sends him two Sicilian peaches that the Emperor eats alone in his cell with a glass of milk.

She wanders aimlessly in the Turin streets, near the Porta Nova Station or along the banks of the Po. Everything she loves has disappeared. From the gutted houses, the cellars, the open churches, an acrid odor of mold wafts out. Sometimes in summer, when it is hot and windy, the smell is so unbearable that she has to cover her mouth with a scarf in order not to vomit.

Towards evening, cart vendors, people who are alone, people in exile come sit on the benches — or what is left of them. They are bored. They are waiting.

For whom?

Pavese claims they are waiting for the city to crumble — the happy apocalypse.

During the long summer vacation, they get together—the usual group of friends—and meet up at the Medieval Castle or the Royal Gardens near the Antonelliana Pier. The group consists of about ten friends more or less the same age, the girls in light summer frocks and bobby socks, the boys in dark suits, ties and elegant sports moccasins — already quite the signorini (young men).

They consume ice-cream *(gelati)*. They smoke American cigarettes. They drink Cinzano. They hold forth about Italy giving voice to prudently disenchanted thoughts. Something is brewing, no doubt about it, in America, in Europe finally freed from the tyrants, but they don't know what it is. In any case, the present is in ruins. The future is a pit of anguish. They stroll along the Po. Some of them hold hands. The crazier ones or the more impatient ones kiss. They are called Gianni, Giorgio, Francesco or Michele. They will become doctors or lawyers, white collar workers or examining magistrates. They will be handsome and idle in a destroyed city. They already have about them that look of the *vitelloni* filmed by the great Fellini.

The sky above the fortress became dark with gliders, as in a Hollywood movie. Some of them crash-land on the rocks; others disappear in the forest. Only two or three manage to land without a problem near the prison.

Then, a commando from Germany, armed and led by Otto Skorzeny, a specialist in high risk operations, demands that the Duce, who has just opened his veins and is resting in the infirmary, be freed. The guards comply. Not a shot is fired. The men leave again, as they arrived, by sending their small silent airplanes back up in the sky.

Two days later in Munich, Mussolini meets Chancellor Hitler, who forces him to return to Italy and reconstitute a fascist government that will prevail, chaotic and pathetic, for nearly nineteen months: it will be the Republic of Salò.

One last time, in November 1943, Campo is to meet with the man for whom he will have worked for more than twelve years; the man whose image he will have produced, reproduced and altered an infinite number of times on post-cards, coins, transfer decals, stamps, military decorations.

This happens on the waterfront of Lake Garda, in one of those rich patrician villas that the owners had abandoned at the beginning of the hostilities and is now occupied by the head of a phantom government.

He is seated at his desk. He is totally focused in the reading of a letter that he is annotating with a red pencil. He doesn't seem to notice Antonio standing in front of him. His vest is unbuttoned, his belt loose. He appears to be in great pain. His left hand seems glued to his stomach and keeps squeezing it. He is worried and tired. He is wearing black-rimmed glasses that make him look older.

"Seven years ago, I was still an interesting personality. Now I am defunct."

With a swoop of the hand, he points at the files that clutter his desk.

"Yes, Campo, I am working. I am keeping busy though I am aware it is all a farce. I am waiting for the play to end. I no longer feel like an actor, I don't feel like an actor anymore, I only feel like the last spectator."

As Antonio prepares to photograph him, the Duce straightens up and, for an instant, resumes the old familiar pose. Campo observes this somber visage, the way he has of putting his hands on his hips and of throwing his head back, and then a feeling of unspeakable disgust rises up in him.

A week later, Campo receives the order to leave for Zagreb where he will be in charge of railroad communications. Nora and the children will soon be joining him.

They will remain here, in Zagreb, until April 1945, in military barracks adjoining the station.

The secret images have been left behind in Turin, under a floorboard on Via Groscavallo.

There isn't much to do for entertainment in Zagreb. There are no balls, no social gatherings, no cinemas with Hollywood films. Every evening is spent at home, in the living room, gathered around the radio.

Programs are broadcast in every language — it is a veritable Tower of Babel!

But how to decide which language can be trusted?

According to the language in which the latest news is reported, be it German, Croatian, English or Italian, the reports are mutually and totally contradictory. The Allies are progressing North, but the Germans are resisting. Italy is in the hands of the partisans, but the Duce is still solidly in control of the power. The American troops have landed in Normandy, but the Germans have pushed them back towards the sea.

No one knows where this absurd war will end. Every night, though, the same song returns, haunting, nerve shattering and heavy with threat and the children pick it up in unison despite Antonio's disapproval:

Una mattina mi sono alzato,
O bella ciao, bella ciao,
Una mattina mi sono alzato,
E ho trovato l'invasor.

O partigiano, porta mi via,
O bella ciao, bella ciao
O partigiano, porta mi via,
Qui mi sento di morir.

E sè io muoio da partigiano,
O bella ciao, bella ciao,

E sè io muoio da partigiano
Tu mi devi seppellir.

E seppellire sulla montagna
O bella ciao, bella ciao
E seppellire sulla montagna
Sott' l'ombra di un bel fior.

Così la gente che passeranno
O bella ciao, bella ciao,
Così la gente che passeranno
Mi diranno "o che bel fiore"

E questo è il fiore del partigiano
O bella ciao, bella ciao,
E questo è il fior del partigiano
Morto per la libertà.

One morning I woke up
O bella ciao, bella ciao,
One morning I woke up
And I found the invader.

Oh partisan, carry me away,
O bella ciao, bella ciao
Oh partisan, carry me away,
For I feel I'm dying.

And if I die as a partisan
O bella ciao, bella ciao
And if I die as a partisan
You have to bury me

But bury me up in the mountain
O bella ciao, bella ciao
But bury me up in the mountain
Under the shadow of a beautiful flower.

And the people who will pass by
O bella ciao, bella ciao,

And the people who will pass by
Will say to me: "what a beautiful flower"

This is the flower of the partisan
O bella ciao, bella ciao,
This is the flower of the partisan
Who died for freedom

Of course Campo is not there to witness the final debacle, when the Emperor as he is attempting to flee to Switzerland (where he had already once found asylum) is arrested by a group of partisans on that April 27th, 1945. He is wearing a German uniform and his bewigged face disappears almost completely under a Wehrmacht cap. He is fleeing Milan in an old truck carrying a load of soldiers in retreat. He is pale and haggard. He doesn't say a word—just barely grumbles a few snatches of German with a heavy accent from Romagna, and offers absolutely no resistance.

The men responsible for his arrest are Pier Luigi Bellini Delle Stelle (alias Pedro, his clandestine partisan name) commander of the brigade, and Urbano Lazzari (alias Bill). They are seen posing side by side in a number of photos in which they are wearing the uniform of the partisans (raw linen trousers, long jacket and, around their necks, a red scarf).

Like two bounty hunters, they take pride in showing off their trophy.

Nora is the one who will discover, on the front page of the morning newspapers, that famous image that will be seen around the world: Mussolini and his mistress, Claretta Petacci, hanging upside down from a beam in a garage on Piazza Loretto in Milan, the very place where fifteen hostages had been shot by the fascists in August of 1944. A closer look shows that la Petacci's skirt has been tied around her legs with a string to prevent it from indecently rolling up to her waist

This is the last image of History: another expiatory sacrifice.

Nora: her sweet look, her silent mouth.

They return to a city in ruins, gutted houses, destroyed bridges, churches sacked.

Everywhere a smell of piss and smoke. Even the sky is heavy with soot.

Not a day goes by that Antonio does not fear for his life. As if, by a cruel reversal, he were no longer behind the camera lens, but in front, at the exact point where the camera is aimed, in the crosshairs of the blind eye.

No longer is he the voyeur of History: the mute and obliging spectator in a game beyond his comprehension. No longer is he the clairvoyant who was able to decipher the future in the silence of his dark room—instead he has become a *vaurien*, a delinquent. He is no longer the hunter of images who is careful about the depth and focus of the shot, but has now turned into the prey.

A book in hand, Campo spends all day walking the streets of Turin. His steps often lead him to the banks of the Po. It is evening. He sits down on a bench. He recites the following lines from Pavese to himself:

Memories begin at night
Blown by the wind to take shape and arise
And to listen to the river's voice.
Water is the same,
In the darkness, as the vanished years.

Night after night he has the same dream: armed partisans burst into his room, they ransack everything, furniture, dishes, radio, antique harmonium and seize the old cardboard boxes where his secret archives are stored (thousands of images of the Duce's life) then, with loud yells, they line up the traitors against the wall before shooting them in the back of their neck.

Turin has now become an open-air city. Crows fly out the windows with a flutter of wings.

Fat black rats have taken over the streets. The thin, charred trees have lost all their leaves. Women stand frozen on the thresholds of destroyed houses staring blankly into space.

It is the law of the victor. As in Dresden, in Cherbourg, in Guernica, unrelenting, deliberate pounding of civilians from the air. Streets once filled with animation, with elegant women, with children riding tricycles, with intelligent, modest and happy men. A hard-working and anxious society.

Who will remember them?

Last night, while new explosions echoed in his head, Antonio slipped out of bed ever so quietly (without waking Nora who slept by his side). He went into the living room and built a big fire in the chimney. He threw his images into the flames with no regrets. The official photos and all the family photos: Nora sitting on the steps of the Taormina Grand Hotel or sunbathing in the gardens of the Parma Casino; Livia running on the beach of Trieste, posing in front of Garibaldi's bust, or licking an ice cream on the quay of Positano. But he never touched the little wooden strong box.

To be sure, things happened: war, bias, even willful blindness. And Antonio allowed himself to be caught up in the game. He played the Emperor's game, of lives of glorious and ridiculous images, of lies raised to the status of truth, of intoxication through photography.

Meanwhile, only a few steps away, there were raids, persecutions, opponents being arrested, pillage of newspapers, violence visited upon the Jews (who were also part of his family).

How could he have kept silent?

Campo has sent Nora and the children away to the country to be with a cousin who farms agricultural land in the Po Valley. Thank goodness! For last night the militiamen stormed the apartment on Via Groscavallo.

There were about a dozen of them, all wearing boots, helmets and carrying guns. They broke down the door. They slammed Antonio against the wall. They went through every room with a fine-tooth comb. They were as enraged as wolves. In a frenzy, they kept searching for something (an image, a proof, a secret) that they never could find.

"You are Campo, the photographer, aren't you?"

Without even giving him time to answer, one of the soldiers struck him with the butt of his gun. He fell to the ground, his mouth bloody. The militiamen went on searching, methodically, savagely. They ripped open the closets: coats, shirts and evening gowns were strewn on the floor; they smashed the radio, knocked over all the furniture. The cleverer ones carried off Antonio's cameras, the magnesium flash bulbs, the emulsions and rolls of film. The others made away with Nora's jewelry.

Livia is rotting in the country between the rice fields that look like marshes and her mother who stands guard at the window, immobile and silent, shaking at the slightest gust of wind.

Like Emily a long time ago, she dreams of the city as well as of another life instead of this clandestine existence so full of misery that she has been leading for the past six months in a farm in the Po valley.

At times, she helps the women who are bent over in the muddy water, though her hands are injured by the clumps of rice she pulls out by fistfuls, and her face assaulted by the wind.

Every time I see the film *Riso Amaro* (*Bitter Rice*), I am reminded of Livia: the harsh work in the rice fields and the rebellion that silently rises until it finally explodes, goaded by the raging exhortations of Silvana Mangano, her chest thrown out in her clinging undershirt, rebel with shock value who has more than one charm in her bag.

The purges continue just about everywhere: they are blind, brutal, unrelenting. They swoop down on the nobodies and those without rank, the alleged accomplices, the personalities with no political responsibilities, the witnesses who stood by and said nothing.

In just a few months, Antonio has lost everything: his job as iconographer, his ransacked apartment, his precious photography equipment — all those priceless images.

As if this weren't enough, he was subjected to endless hours of interrogation while the partisans spat on him, brutally beat him, tried to blackmail him, abused him and subjected him to other humiliations before finally dragging him back to his cell in the small hours of the morning.

What is it Antonio is accused of?

Quite simply, of having seen. Or rather of having made images that glorified the fascist regime knowing full well what he was doing. Of having contributed to this imaginary mythology (the discipline, the virile strength, the will of steel), pure figment of the Emperor's imagination, without ever having questioned it, decrying its lie or denouncing it.

Of having been complicit, after all, in the subject matter of his photos. But what he is accused of, more than anything, is his silence: Antonio saw, he saw everything, he was always there where it happened, right in the pulsating center of History, in the mind and brain of the monster, yet he never said a word.

Buried in the country under an assumed name, living with a peasant family of the Po valley, Nora and Livia wallow in silence and abject terror.

Now, not one night goes by when they don't lie in wait for the police van to come and carry them both off to prison.

In summer, in the light from the dormer-window, Livia installs herself to read for hours on end in the middle of eucalyptus, in the silence and heat that turns the attic into a large tropical greenhouse. She loves to be alone, she loves books and quiet.

What she finds up there, far from the city and its noises, is a child's voice that resembles hers, a high, tinny, singing voice, the voice of an invisible child, a voice that knows no age and will always remain a child's voice.

He went home, on a fine April morning, to the devastated apartment.

A mangy dog, sprawled across the threshold, bares its teeth when Antonio approaches, then runs off with a growl. The apartment reeks of smoke and mold, the rug is saturated with the smell of urine. Campo immediately proceeds to the living room. A floor board is raised.

Suddenly his hands start shaking. He is unable to control his fear.

Using a screwdriver, he manages to pop open the resisting slat of wood. He slips his arm in the opening. Praise the Lord! It is still there, the little wooden strong box with the secret images! It is covered with moss and dust.

Campo quickly hides it under his gabardine, and disappears.

The march of the women dressed in black in the rice fields, aprons tied around their waist, barefoot, doubled over in the swampy water as, without exchanging a word, they pull up the long brown razor sharp stems that rise above the water.

Stationed in the shadow behind the attic's window pane, Livia observes the women in the fields with the utmost delight. She takes pleasure in situating herself on the margin of life. Never does she feel freer than up there in her hiding place. Never can the world belong to her more completely.

One morning in September, when she caught sight of that tall thin silhouette on the dirt path, advancing with a slow and measured step, a black briefcase under his arm, at first, Livia did not recognize him.

The man was probably not quite sure of his final destination, for he stopped several times to ask for directions. Then, without raising his head, he set out again walking towards the farm surrounded by spindle trees.

A name rang out in the living-room; his name, again and again. Livia shot out of her hiding place, scrambled down the stairs, and within seconds she had jumped into the arms of her father.

Antonio has brought *frittelle* and a bottle of amaretto from Turin. He is as moved as his daughter Livia. Nora, stunned, stares at her husband. He says that everything is fine, but he doesn't mention the prison.

When Livia asks him if they are going home, the photographer turns pale.

"But…we don't have a home anymore!"

No more images, no, never again.

Alone in the huge empty apartment, Campo drowns himself in music.

He has repaired the harmonium (it hadn't excessively suffered from the militia's fury) and this is where, from now on, he will spend his days. His fingers are stiff. He has to start all over again from ground zero. He practices frenetically. He is eager and impatient, like a child deprived of his music for much too long.

On Sundays, as in the old days in Trieste, he comes to play the organ at the church of the exiled Vaudois of the Piemonte in Corso Vittorio.

The pastor knows Antonio well. He is a short man in his fifties with a round debonaire face who always wears black. He is aware of Antonio's past, his craze for images. He is also aware that his children and his wife are safely hidden somewhere out in the country.

In fact, the pastor himself takes him aside one day after the Sunday service. He shows him a newspaper clipping.

"Turin is a dangerous city, Campo. For you, for your family..."

Then, a moment of silence.

"What's more, four mouths to feed during these times of misery can't be easy!"

He points at a classified ad.

"Look at this! In Switzerland, they are in need of nurses, caretakers, cleaning ladies. It is honest and well paid work. I actually have an address, it is in Nyon on Lake Geneva. I could write a recommendation for Livia."

Tonight for the last time, she came to sit in her favorite spot in the middle of shawls and wool throws under the window, in a corner of her room though far enough from the walls to allow light to fall on her book from every side without being too bright.

"Tomorrow, freedom..."

Livia remained there the entire night, nestled in the feather pillows, reading, gazing up at the sky, shivering with fear.

In Livia's pocket, there is a sheet of paper carefully folded in four on which is written an address, a handful of coins, a small *panettone* — and that's all. She is setting out for the unknown: that land of plenty that somehow managed to escape the great butchery.

"The only country without Hitler."

She doesn't know a word of French. She doesn't know a soul. She has no diploma to speak for her, not even a name where she might find a helping hand.

Like Nora, the foreigner, she is always at the beginning of her story.

X

When she arrives on the quay of the Nyon train station, September 6, 1946, Livia is taken aback by the silence: not many people in the streets, no car noises, quite a change from home, over there, on the other side of the mountains, and no children shouting, no loud blaring of popular songs from transistor radios.

Could there be people actually living here in Switzerland?

Livia is far from the only one to alight from the Milan train on that Monday, September 6, 1946.

There are about a dozen of these young women, all of them Italian, all of them foreigners, all of them barely out of childhood. Some of them come from Puglia or Calabria others from Naples or Sicily; there are peasants from Friuli or the Aosta Valley, girls from the Romagna countryside, students from Tuscany.

Some of these girls speak an obscure dialect that Livia doesn't understand.

Barely have they set foot on the quay on this late summer afternoon, that the police stop them for questioning. A deep hush descends upon the scene. Suitcases are set down with shaky hands. A passport or an identity paper in its stead is produced. Slowly and carefully, a police officer marks it with the saving stamp, countersigns it without a word or smile, and then adds a date fraught with menace.

They are made to line up in two rows on the quay: the one on the right is comprised of all the young women whose papers are in order; the one on the left is an assembly of those who are banished, the negligent ones, the cheaters, the foreigners who are not wanted. They are immediately made to board the next train scheduled to leave for Italy.

Once this first selection has been completed, the police officers escort the young women to a military tent erected on the Perd-Temps square. There, nurses in white coats order them to get undressed.

"Sanitary inspection."

Like her fellow countrywomen, Livia complies. She is embarrassed, she would like to run away, get back on the train that would take her home. But, like the others, she takes off her clothes, puts them down on her suitcase, stands up very straight, hands on her chest once she is naked.

A doctor examines them, one after the other. They are told to spread their legs and to raise their arms above their head. He measures their height and examines them with a stethoscope pressed against their breasts. He runs his hand between their legs, under their armpits, through their hair. He orders them to bend over and, as they catch hold of their ankles with their hands, he examines their anus.

Once he has finished with his inspection, the doctor signals it by nodding his head. A nurse then comes forward; she takes the young woman by the arm and pulls her over to the showers. There, still under the watchful eyes of the nurse, she is made to scrub her body with a disinfecting soap that smells like ammonia, and to wash her hair with a thick black shampoo, supposedly meant to discourage lice.

Two hours later, it is all over. Washed, deloused, purified, but, more than anything, humiliated, they leave the military tent, one by one.

This is where they say their good-byes: some are going to work at the Sangal pasta factory (where a large number of female personnel is employed): others at the match factory behind the train station; and finally, others are destined to work at a psychiatric clinic, La Métairie, where nurses and health-aids are being recruited.

The foreign young woman followed the railroad tracks, walked on a narrow winding path in the middle of tall grass. She walked on for a mile or two, almost without pausing, accompanied by the delicious aroma of lime-blossoms and sage, she went through an ash tree grove and then she reached the clinic.

It is a former manor, built in 1857, with pink plastered walls and windows crowned with triangular gables. The tiled roof is dotted with skylights, every one of them has bars.

A month after his release from prison, Antonio was set up with a new job, working for the railroad.

It is a pencil pusher's life — no ambition and no surprises — in an office reeking of tobacco smoke overlooking the Piazza Garibaldi. Everybody now smokes MS filters, it is the latest fad, and you light them with a Diamond match. Wishing to add a touch of elegance, Antonio uses a cigarette holder. The political police has forgotten about him, as have his friends and his former clients: no one is left who might recognize his name. And Nora, after just a few weeks, has joined him, together with the children, in an apartment with high ceilings, dark lofty rooms, overlooking an inside courtyard; it isn't very far from the small Porta Susa transit train station for all travelers going to Switzerland.

Julien is out of the hospital. He goes from door to door selling laundry soaps, parish newspapers, postcards, all kinds of articles crafted by the blind. He thus travels the length and the breadth of the city with his white cane. He comes across numerous *bistrots* in his travels, and never ignores a single one. This is where he gets together once again with his old mates from the Diamond. None of them work anymore. They spend the afternoon playing cards or forecasting the probable outcomes of the weekend soccer matches.

"This year, the Lausanne-Sports has become stronger and will beat the living daylights out of those pretentious underlings from the end of the lake."

Sometimes, when his friends allow him enough free time, Julien rings the bells of the houses on the lake. It is the Swiss-German maid who comes to the door for Madame is not at home. He sings the praises of his soaps or the good luck charms, the laundry detergent in flakes, which he carries in his satchel.

The young woman listens to his sales-spiel mouth wide open, eyes filled with fear. Needless to say, she doesn't understand a word of what he is saying.

He is far from an ordinary street peddler, Julien, for he cannot see the wares he is trying to sell.

How many times did the secret child walk with him on his rounds?

He always followed the same path, from the Rue de la Gare to the alleys of Rive, where he had drinks with his friends, the Pirates, then, the wharf, the stroll under the plane trees along the lake, the Beau-Rivage hotel and the garden with flowers in full bloom, the music Conservatory, then the beautiful villas almost floating on the water.

Despite his best oratory efforts, it was a miracle if Julien was able to sell anything. People had no real need for anything. They took us for Gypsies, for receivers of stolen goods. If they ever bought laundry soap or key-chains, it was only out of Christian charity. Julien did not appreciate that. He would become angry, would walk off right in the middle of the bargaining process. A dog would run after us all the way to the front gate. I would pull on Julien's arm to prevent him from falling into the flower beds or walk into the bars of the entrance gate.

Once we were out of reach, we would burst into peals of laughter.

At the Métairie, the atmosphere is bizarre, with the muted light filtered through the cotton curtains, that particular medicinal odor that constantly permeates the air in the rooms and most of all, the silence, a disturbing, absolute silence that resembles the silence one finds in cemeteries.

For the foreigner, everything is new. Nothing is at all like what she has imagined: absent are screams of patients, soothing walks in the park, successful recoveries. The patients remain inside their rooms. They are kept out of sight, in secret and in shame, as if they had the plague. They no longer have a face. They never greet a soul and don't even react when they catch sight of their own reflection in the mirror.

Only a chosen few are allowed to go out, the healthier ones, the very well-to-do patients.

They can be seen walking the halls like ghosts; their eyes are lifeless, a cigarette is forever glued to their lips. Amongst the nurses, there are whispers that here you can find finance stars, singers suffering from depression, seriously damaged politicians—and even the daughter of an Italian dictator who ended up hanging from the beam of a garage.

She lives in a garret, like the other nurses, a room with a bed, a sink under a mirror, and an armchair covered in tired velvet. The toilet is at the end of the hall. It only flushes properly half of the time.

On certain evenings, you can almost make out her furtive silhouette behind the curtains. Her face is turned to the window. Her body is sunk into the armchair. She contemplates the lake with empty green eyes.

On her lap lies a book, open, but face down, its cover shining in the darkness.

For the foreigner, books are precious friends. The things she confides to them, the secrets she reveals to them, the troubles and joys she entrusts to them, all of these they carefully keep to themselves, in the folds of their pages, without ever betraying them or giving them away. Books are always within reach, in her bag, faithful and readily available. They are guardians of silence and memory. They keep death at bay. Their soft and melodious voice can only be heard by those who know how to listen for it.

And yet she is also free to close her book at any given moment, free to leave a friend for another at her slightest whim, free to return later to her original text, to pick up where she left off, without ever being in danger of provoking an argument.

Like Antonio, her father, the foreigner is a quick learner. Difficult patients are entrusted to her, and she takes care of them diligently. It is delicate work, not without risk, but this does not frighten Livia. She becomes especially attached to the patients who have come for sleep therapy, either because they are exhausted, or depressed, or suicidal. She loves plunging them into a deep artificial sleep, taking care of them during all those days and nights, of which they will retain no memory, and finally waking them up as if she were bringing the dead back to life.

First, a tube is inserted through the nose, until it reaches the stomach; then the gastric juice is pumped out with a syringe. The juice is applied to a piece of litmus paper that turns imperceptibly from blue to pink. The syringe is removed. A sort of funnel is attached to the tube, then a syrup is poured into it, adapted to the quantity of insulin that has been injected and saturated with sugar. The tube is removed. It takes several minutes (sometimes much longer) before the patient wakes up.

During this process, the patient sweats profusely, his eyelids flutter convulsively, his hands are clenched.

When the patient comes to, they change him as well as the soaked sheets, they rub him down with camphorated alcohol, they speak to him softly in order not to frighten him, and let him adapt progressively to light.

Most often, after a week of sleep therapy the patient eats a meal with a hearty appetite.

Never, in her first life, had Livia ever imagined that the world might be divided into two: on the one hand, are the patients, on the other, the hordes of white coats who minister to them.

Those who are mad and their wardens.

That the latter have the power of life or death over the former who outnumber them by far.

Pierre is twenty, the worst age of all. Three times in the past, have his parents sent him to a sanatorium. He was given medication to keep him quiet. On unsteady legs, he walked through the hallways, took the pathways in the yard and once again managed to climb over the walls of his prison. He doesn't really walk with his feet on the ground. He is spaced out, his eyes unfocused, drifting beyond the clouds. He speaks to no one. He doesn't respond to any form of greeting. He is blind to the women who smile at him. He is still unable to weep.

In his room on the second floor, he is on the alert for the slightest noise in the hallway.

Constantly at the ready, he is on the lookout for a glance or a voice, he is waiting for the one who is coming to save him. He doesn't know her face. He has not seen her yet, not even in the park or in the hallways.

But her voice is familiar. As if he had always known her.

One day, he was brought to a small room: olive-green walls, no windows, light coming from a fixture in the ceiling, no furniture besides a narrow berth-type bed. Black leather straps, metal handcuffs, bright screen monitors.

They forced him down on the berth. Pierre struggled. Two men in white coats immobilized him, pinned him down and tied him up with straps around his legs and wrists. They stuck his head in a sort of helmet, between two screws that dug into his skin. He tried to scream.

At that moment, a young nurse put a piece of rubber in his mouth. She was beautiful and silent. He tried to scream again, but his scream stuck in his throat. Now he can't breathe or swallow his own saliva.

Above his head, like ghosts, the doctors move around him and they are all speaking at once.

"How much shall we start out with?

"120, just to get an idea."

It feels like an explosion. A storm in his head, a burning sensation runs through his muscles. His body arches. He bites down on the rubber. His eyes roll up in their sockets.

They untie him. Even after several minutes, he hasn't moved. He plays dead on his berth, foaming at the mouth, muscles on fire.

"It is over."

They bring him back to his own room on the second floor, and lay him down on his bed. He remains flat on his back, eyes staring up at the ceiling. He does not utter a word. The storm inside his head has turned into a kind of fire. Yes, a forest fire.

When he opens his eyes again, in the white light, he has a fleeting sense — like a flash — of recognizing a nurse who is smiling at him. But he can be sure of nothing. He has become nothing.

The foreigner is naïve. Her French isn't very good yet, and she lets some of the patients, the sly tearful ones, take advantage of her as they try to kiss her on the mouth, let their hands wander in the folds of her white coat.

In the same way she has learned silence, Livia learns obedience: she obeys the doctors who treat the nurses like servants; she obeys the rich and capricious patients (you must absolutely not upset them in any way), and finally she obeys Mademoiselle Meyer — the warden — who constantly makes fun of Livia because of her accent.

For days and weeks, he says absolutely nothing. He just sits without moving in his bed (it has bars like a crib or a cell), arms crossed, staring fixedly at some particular spot above the door.

At a crucifix? or at the skylight with the crossbars?

He never opens his mouth except to eat.

Fists clenched, eyes turned inward, the secret child lies perfectly still. He is free, however, when it strikes his fancy, to explore his glorious interior landscapes, to climb the tallest mountains, to sail the distant seas while his abandoned remains are left behind, lying inert and silent, down here, in a corner of the room.

His ruse now consists of pretending to be like all the others.

Here, in Pierre's room, is where, on a Sunday in May, they meet for the second time. First, she thinks that he, in his paleness and silence, looks handsome.

For a brief moment, Livia even manages to catch his eye. The man rests his eyes on her.

His lips quiver. He is going to speak. But just when he is about to open his mouth, when the words tumble over each other on his tongue, a torrent held back far too long, a voice rings out in the hallway, a sharp inflexible voice, Mademoiselle Meyer, and the man falls back into his silence.

Here is the image that is imprinted that day: a young woman, strikingly beautiful, walking towards him as if carried by a breeze, long legs above flat heels, looking serious, eyes of an unforgettable green, full lips, dark hair falling in waves on her half-open coat.

These two are now foreigners as they face each other. Foreign to each other, and foreign mostly to the world around them: this is probably what draws them together from the outset, as if they were speaking a same language. Solitude and silence. The feeling of not belonging.

One night, he left his room, moved by who knows what kind of crazy desire: yes, to see the foreigner once more, to see her face for a second, just one image, just one second, to surprise the foreigner in her room. He climbed the stairs without a sound, and placed himself behind the door.

From the doorway he can only see her back: Livia is naked down to her waist, bent over an earthenware bowl, her hair wet and soapy. She is not alone. Another woman standing behind her, pouring lukewarm water on her head, is a participant in the ceremony.

When she straightens up, it is a game, Livia throws her hair back and splashes the whole room, and the other woman, near the stove, laughs and protects herself as best she can. Suddenly, Livia turned around, but too late: Pierre is already facing her. Her smile freezes. She looks at him with terror. The other woman lets out a muffled cry.

With an awkward gesture, she crosses her hands on her chest.

The clinic is a place of secrets. Some patients are detained in their rooms for months on end — or even years — by suspicious heirs. Their mail is censored. Their phone calls are filtered. They are allowed visitors selectively. Livia, then, plays the fearless messenger by forwarding letters to mysterious addressees, by sneaking in forbidden packages. The terrible Meyer is never far away, but she never manages to catch the foreigner red-handed.

Other patients choose to hole up in the shadows, some to escape the pack of creditors, others to abort (or give birth) clandestinely; others yet to attempt one last time to rid themselves of an addiction to alcohol or cocaine; others, finally, to have their face reshaped until it is unrecognizable, which will allow them to begin a second life.

Her favorite patient is a famous humorist who has written hundreds of songs (some of them are dedicated to his beautiful nurse), who has published columns on moods and emotions in several newspapers (the well-known *"Bonjour"*), and written dozens of skits and plays. His satirical genius is acknowledged by everyone, except by himself. He excels, it would seem, in the art of self-sabotage, but also in delusions of grandeur. His stays are frequent, and low profile. At every stay, he always demands Livia. He wants to be treated and coddled only by her. She is the only one who can reason with him. The only one, as well, from whom he will graciously accept reprimands or advice.

"Livia, I'm so tired! If only I could get some sleep…

Then Livia does what is necessary to immerse the depressed entertainer in the deepest sleep. "Good bye, Mademoiselle!"

When he wakes up two weeks later, he is a new man, ready to go back to the cruel world of reality.

"I feel refreshed, like a young man, Livia! Thanks to you!"

And, as he lifts his gown:

"Look at that — I'm hard!"

But their most famous boarder — the most secret, too — is a young Italian woman, tall and slender, about forty years old, her hair cut short, gamine style, who seems to have kept from her masculine upbringing an excellent control of her emotions and an intractable spirit of rebellion.

All by herself, she occupies an entire wing of the *chalet,* one of the three buildings of the clinic. She never speaks to anyone, never receives visitors, and lives as a recluse in her room. The secret surrounding her (what exactly is the name of her illness?) is well kept, and her name is never uttered inside of the clinic's walls. Sometimes, at night, Livia catches a glimpse of her face, of her figure, behind the bay-window of the chalet. She paces up and down in her room, speaks out loud to herself, has sudden fits of anger or of crying.

One day, Livia approached her room, overriding the rules of prudence and discretion. The door is half-open. Livia knocks lightly, then walks into the room where an apocalyptic mess prevails. In front of her, the young woman, holding a knife, is striking out at the air with rage, her eyes dilated with hatred, making as if to stab an invisible enemy.

"A morte! Traditore!"

As soon as she sees Livia, the young woman freezes in terror. She collapses into a wing chair, drops her knife, cradles her face in her hands.

"Are you okay, Mademoiselle?"

The young woman is still talking to herself, in a mixture of Romagna and Tuscan dialects, ghosts are dancing before her eyes, a man in a military uniform, hands in his pockets, a smile on his lips, shouting, "Long live Italy!" at that very moment, the officer commanding the firing squad gives the order to fire, then she sees a short man with a shaved head, her idol, her father, chin up, fist resting on his hip, at whose feet she throws herself sobbing, begging for mercy for her husband.

"Assassino!"

Standing in the middle of the room, Livia is petrified.

The young woman looks at her for a long moment, with her green empty eyes, but she does not recognize her.

Livia has never met her, but she has seen her picture hundreds of times, sometimes in the *gente* section of the newspapers, sometimes in Antonio's files. She is the one who married Count Ciano, on April 24, 1930, at the San Giuseppe church, on Via Nomentana in Rome, who was then sent to Shanghai, China with her handsome ambassador of a husband, where she became the talk of the town, by hanging around gaming tables for days and endless nights, betting and losing monstrous amounts of money and contracting debts she was in no position to pay. She is also the one, Livia remembers, who turned out to be among the first Italian women to drive an automobile, to wear trousers, to flaunt herself in a sports outfit (short skirt, bathing suit showing her bare arms and legs), the very one whom her parents one day nicknamed the *cavallina matta* (the crazy filly), because of her unpredictable temperament and how uninterested she was in her studies.

Another image shows Livia in her nurse's uniform (light-blue dress, little white apron), sitting in a chaise lounge. Her hair is drawn back. Her eyes and lips are painted. She is smiling at the camera.

It is Sunday, day of rest, but Livia is on call. Behind her, at the back of a shadowed courtyard, you can make out the clinic entrance, the heavy curtains drawn, the rooms securely locked — an oppressive, threatening atmosphere.

On the second floor, behind metal bars, is Pierre's ghost.

Other ghosts haunt the forbidden wing of the *chalet*.

Upbraided by that Meyer woman, Livia no longer dares approach Edda Ciano, Signorina Mussolini. She continues, however, to lurk in the vicinity of her room. Close enough to hear the shouts, the crash of broken glass, streams of curses in Romagna dialect, the sound of blows against the wall.

In the letters she sends every week to her parents, Livia talks about her work, about the clinic on the lake and about the strange boarder, a recluse in her room, about this new country that she finds austere and beautiful, and whose language she is trying to learn. But she does not talk about Pierre, not a word, not an allusion: he is her very own secret that belongs only to her.

Twice again, Livia crosses paths with Edda, the crazy filly.

The first time, she came across her unexpectedly in the park, on a summer night; she was wandering in her night gown, her hair down, scratches on her face, and she was angry with someone in the shadows, shouting insults at this person you couldn't see.

"*Vigliacco!*"

As soon as she saw Livia, Edda relaxed, she looked at her with eyes that were deep luminous pools, then, unsteadily, she walked towards her, as if she knew her.

"Did you recognize me?"

— "Yes, Mademoiselle."

Edda Ciano smiled at her.

"You are the last person to see my real face."

As Livia was frowning, the young woman added:

"Whatever happens, Signorina, don't forget to forget me!"

In Turin, life returns to normal. Difficult, Nora writes, to relearn how to live in a city full of ruins and tears. Your closest friends have disappeared. Day and night you can hear the noise of the mechanical diggers clearing away the rubble. Turin is a town of ghosts and ashes. Food is expensive, and Antonio's salary from the railroad is barely enough to sustain the four hungry mouths of the household. Pierrette has just turned twenty. The suitors are falling over each other at her feet. But the young woman hardly deigns to grace them with a look or a smile, or a word of encouragement.

In the photo, you can see Pierrette surrounded by boys, it is winter and snow is piled up in drifts against the tree trunks, she has a man's felt hat on her head, slightly tilted as is the fashion at the time, and her curly hair falls in waves on her shoulders. A woolen scarf in shaded tones hangs like a tie on her chest. She is wearing a long coat and leather boots. Livia can barely recognize her sister in this elegant young woman.

As for Elvire, she has just won the figure skating Championship. She is wearing the usual female skating outfit: flesh-colored tights, short frilly skirt and glittery top. The picture is a little blurry because Elvire is doing a particularly difficult figure, and is focusing all her strength in that effort. You can make out, at the edge of the picture, clusters of impressed spectators.

Paul, the little one, has just celebrated his twelfth birthday. He is starting junior high, but he does not like school.

Who took those pictures? Antonio? Nora? Some anonymous admirer?

The story does not tell.

It has been two years since Antonio took an oath never again to touch a camera. He has been trying to respect his promise, but, naturally, temptation is strong.

And something inside him forces him to respond to those faces and voices from the outside.

For Pierre, love is a sacred image: an icon.

He never tells a soul about it. It is his most intimate and most frightening secret.

And especially not Emilie who would want to know everything, as usual, about the lucky girl, her name and her face, the state of her finances, the way she dresses, the brand of her perfume, the color of her eyes, of her dresses, of her lipstick, Emilie who would want to meet her and then would immediately ply her with advice and introduce her to Julien who would sweet-talk her with his charmer's voice, would overwhelm her with compliments on her beauty and the color of her nail polish, he who can't ever see anything farther than his fingertips.

Livia likes books and pastries, great opera arias, words in the Italian language, Gene Kelly and musicals, putting her patients to sleep, going for walks along the Po with her sisters, Antonio's smile in the morning when he has had his fill of images, rabbit and polenta, the *Divina Comedia* and *I Promessi Sposi,* long drives at night in sports cars, light and sparkling Asti champagne, Renaissance painters; she likes serving others, helping, being unobtrusive, belonging, vegetable noodle soup, nights of endless dancing in ball rooms, delicious *moretti* that you savor at around one in the afternoon at the Torrefazione Beccuti, via Pietro Micca, parties and birthdays, American music.

Pierre likes balls and sports cars, dancing with pretty girls, playing soccer or basketball on Perd-Temps square, Emilie's *malakoffs*, Glenn Miller or Duke Ellington's hits, tongue with caper sauce, going from *carnotzet* to *carnotzet* (those rooms the Swiss set aside for drinking with friends, usually in the cellar) to taste the white wine from la Côte, silence, mountain cabins, planes, Julien's strange pictures, the cheese you eat in Jura cooperative cheese dairies, parties and birthdays.

The last time Livia met Edda Ciano was in September 48, at the end of summer.

That day, Livia had to stand in for another nurse in the operating room. She recognized her right away, strapped down to the narrow leather bench-like bed, wearing a white gown, her hair tied back in a kind of blue net, the skin of her face pulled back, tight as a drum.

"Don't forget what I told you!"

Sleep is overcoming her features, she is trying to smile, one last struggle to say a few words: "Soon, I will no longer exist."

The surgery goes well: Edda's features are rubbed out; the curve of her nose is corrected; her lips are patiently redrawn with a scalpel; her smile, her childish rebellious face is entirely remodeled.

Whenever he goes on his rounds to peddle his wares, Julien never leaves his little Rollei behind. He strolls through the city, crosses the Marketplace, stops in the café next to the fountain to quench his thirst. And there, he remains for long moments, on the lookout for a voice, birds singing in a tree, a woman singing to herself in the street.

He aims his camera in the direction of the voice or of the birds, without being able to make out a living soul in the viewfinder and he presses the shutter release. The angle of the shot is often audacious, dizzying high-angle and stunning low-angle shots because the photographer is blind.

Often, Julien manages to include himself in the photo, but only in the negative: as a shadow more or less distorted, as a ghost with huge black arms, ready to swoop down in an instant on the prey he desires.

They meet in secret, every night, near the railroad tracks…

Livia who is often on night duty, has gone through the rooms to ensure that each patient has taken his pills for the night, the sleeping pills and tranquilizers, the placebos and neuroleptics, making sure that all the lights are out, and that silence reigns on each floor. After that, she has gone to see those patients who have been plunged into an insulin shock. She has checked their pulses, raised their eyelids, and made sure they were sleeping peacefully. She has left the building through the kitchen giving a biscuit to the dog, Fela, so that she won't growl.

In his room, Pierre has quietly bided his time. A nurse has come by (it is not Livia) to give him his dose of sedative, he has put the pills in his mouth, smiled, pretended to swallow, blinked as a sign of obedience, then has sunk back into his bed, yawned, as the nurse has slowly left the room, then he has spat out the sleeping pills into his handkerchief.

He has gotten up, dressed quickly, looked out of the window at the shining night, the beautiful rays of the moon illuminating the lime and oak trees in the park. He has remained behind the door for a few moments, listening for any noise in the corridor, then he has gone down the stairs. He has opened the door. He is in the courtyard. He has raised his eyes and looked at the sky.

Last night, Livia dreamt about Turin: she is with Antonio and Pierre, in front of a large church, in a café on Piazza della Consolata. The two men are quietly talking about this and that as they enjoy a *bicerin*. Served in a wine glass, this is an espresso with added cocoa powder, liquid crème fraîche and a spoonful of sugar.

Livia, upon awakening, has a delicious taste in her mouth: the bitterness of both the chocolate and the coffee, the sweetness of the sugar, the freshness of the cream—an unforgettable marriage.

It is the story of my life that I am trying to find: two streams (two currents, two desires), who, on a given day, at a specific point in time and space for some secret reason, have mingled their waters: me.

Everything that I am writing is authentic. It is what I have been told: it is made up of fables, of real-life legends, and of anecdotes gathered through the years and the encounters.

Like all memories, everything that I am writing is therefore authentically false.

Through the night until early morning, they talk, they kiss, but they do not touch.

They cannot hear the secret child who is howling within them.

They have so much to say to each other, so many secrets to share, wishes, laughs, fears, and tears to confess!

Who has brought them here? And why?

How to explain the miracle of their meeting?

They make no promises or eternal vows of love. They don't have time for that. They are sitting at the foot of a tree, in the early morning, they gaze at the lake, at the mountains that are beginning to gleam in the morning light, Yvoire, over there, like a handful of stars, they listen to the North wind singing in the trees, they gaze around them and within each other, they smile, they fall silent, they cannot believe their eyes.

Pierre has finally been discharged from the clinic. His freedom only lasts a few days. Under pressure from Emilie, he has become an apprentice to an electrician from Nyon whose shop on the Rue de la Gare, is one of the finest in town.

His master, a stern and suspicious man, watches him closely night and day.

Every morning, he is there, on the threshold of his shop, making sure all the apprentices arrive right on time. And in the evening, he is the last person to leave the shop, not without having previously searched each apprentice, to rest assured that the latter is not carrying away anything of value in his pockets.

Pierre bears the patron's mistrust without flinching. He doesn't say a word, allowing not even a hint of revolt to transpire. For long months, he learned how to turn his silence into a weapon.

And his life is somewhere else.

Saturday at the clinic is a regular day. Some patients are allowed to go out. A car comes to pick them up, unobtrusively, behind the pavilion. They spend the weekend with their family until they return to their room on Sunday night before beginning a new round of treatments. The others, those who have no one to claim them, stay shut away in their rooms.

Since Livia is a foreigner, she is often on night duty. She watches over her patients like a mother. She measures out the doses of the sleeping pills and tranquilizers as she pleases. She is the guardian of sleep.

Once she has finished her rounds, she slips away like a shadow. She is the one that can be seen, after midnight, walking through the park without a sound and leaving by the small wrought iron door that opens up on the road to the lake.

At the Beau-Rivage, droves of suitors are already waiting for her, huddled around the sideboard. The bolder ones invite her to dance. As she refuses, some of them become angry, their eyes red from the white wine.

Fortunately, a young handsome man comes to her rescue: he is dressed like a prince, with black, combed-back hair, a devastating smile and a cigarette dangling from his lips. She lets him carry her off. Laughter and grumbling abound. The suitors are greatly vexed.

They dance all night long.

When they can't be together, on the other days of the week, they write each other.

At noon or in the evening, in his bed, in his feverish handwriting, Pierre writes dozens of letters that he goes to slip in person in the clinic mailbox, just before setting out for work (for, in his opinion, the mail is too slow).

With an unpleasant grimace, Miss Meyer distributes the mail every day, at noon on the dot, and makes ironic remarks concerning these missives that bear no stamp. Livia could not care less because her life is somewhere else. She waits until she is alone to open the letter and she can at last read those words that move her so deeply every time. She counts the hours until the evening, when, in the solitude of her room under the roof, in the deep and silent night, she reads the letter from Pierre over and over, and then hurries to answer him, in his own language, she tells him about herself, her story, her strange life without roots, her exile, her pain, everything she has never dared reveal to anyone else.

How many ghosts inhabit these letters!

The secret child, like a vampire, devours their juices. He does not miss a word. He feeds on this music, forever new and amazing. He knows that love, at its very beginning, can hang in the balance of just a few words.

Where is Livia's life?

Who does it belong to?

Every month now, Nora's letters become increasingly urgent.

"We miss you so much, *carissima figlia!* Our Petit Paul — who has become a handsome thirteen-year-old — is impatient to see you again. And Antonio! He is pining for you a little more with each passing day. He misses his first-born daughter. He searches for her everywhere, in his dreams, along the river Po, in the photos from before the war. It is an open wound."

Livia takes her own sweet time before answering. She wants to gain some extra time. But the missives from Italy become more insistent, more imperious with every passing day:

"Come quickly!"

When she gets to Porta Susa, that noisy and smoky train station, Livia feels strange: she recognizes every stone of the quay, the huge glass panes black with soot, the cries of the hawkers.

She has come home, to her good old city of Turin, and yet, she has come as a foreigner.

The entire family — no one is missing — has come to welcome her: Antonio in a dark suit, necktie with a large bow and white carnation in the buttonhole; Nora in a flower-print dress, a hat with a little veil and matching gloves; Pierrette and Elvire, more young ladylike than ever; and Paul — little Paul! — in an *alpino* uniform.

That evening, in the big apartment of Via Groscavallo, what a celebration! Nora has prepared home-made soup, *saltimbocca* with vegetables, *knödel* with cherries drowned in a voluptuous bath of melted butter and cinnamon, and *crème brulée*.

That night — and the following, and again the one after that — Livia lies awake, unable to fall asleep.

In order to let light into her heart, she writes every night to Pierre, troubled and fiery letters. But writing doesn't make anything brighter. She creates ghosts. She adds a shade of darkness to the night.

And in the morning, once she has mailed her letter, Livia feels more lost and alone than ever.

With every passing day, with every letter, Pierre is going out of his mind. He can no longer bear his master. He is becoming quarrelsome. He is neglectful of his work. His parents, who are still lodging him, don't know what to do. No matter what they say, what advice they give, or what they threaten, nothing seems to make the slightest difference. Nothing touches his elusive soul. His mood is flighty and constantly changing, He seems to be a foreigner in his own life.

Then one day, without alerting a soul, neither his parents, nor his master, nor his friends, he is off and on his way to Turin.

In his pockets, Livia's last letter with a return address written in red, a handful of coins, and a map of the city. He doesn't speak a blessed word of Italian. Once there, he doesn't know a soul. He has to sort it out on his own.

Just like Livia, the foreigner, he is forever at the beginning of his story.

When he arrives on the quay of the Porta Susa train station, Pierre can't believe the noise. How crowded the streets are! Fancy cars, street peddlers, transistor radios blaring out the latest *canzoni* of the hit parade.

With only pennies in his pocket, Pierre proceeds to the address on the envelope: Via Groscavallo 23. The sky is empty and dirty. Entire neighborhoods are in ruins. Shadows eat away at the peeling facades.

Here it is.

How his finger trembles when he rings the golden doorbell!

No answer.

With a beating heart, he presses the bell anew.

A window lights up on the ground floor, someone draws the curtains, voices buzz in the darkness. Then a door opens slightly. Footsteps resound in the inside courtyard.

Panic stricken, Pierre disappears in the night.

He walks blindly through the dark and silent streets. He has lost all his arrogance. Livia's face still floats in front of his eyes, but it is beginning to blur. Her features are more and more scrambled. They are mixed up with the ghosts of the past.

On Via Pietro Micca, there is a large café that stays open all night. But, at that hour, only a few tables are occupied. Pierre installs himself all the way in the back of the café, chair against the mirror, near a jukebox that is softly playing a song by Milva. He orders a *moretto*. The cup they bring him looks like a tiered wedding cake, with its sculpted foam sprinkled with powdered cocoa rising above the burning mixture of coffee and chocolate.

Near the counter, there are postcards arranged on a metallic turntable. Pierre picks one out: it shows the banks of the Po river, in the evening, dark with people out for a stroll, with the Capuccin Mount rising in the background, like a Chinese shadow play. He starts writing. Words flow from his pen like a silent river. And Livia's face, because of this magic, recovers its former clear features, her aqua green eyes, her long hair with its autumn colors.

On the juke box, Domenico Modugno, the Italian crooner, has replaced Milva.

The following day, when he slides his postcard under the heavy carriage door to the building, day has not yet begun to break. In a strange way, Pierre is light-hearted. His love is more powerful than time, borders, or languages.

There are days, in the morning while the sun is still young, when he feels compelled to respond to a silent call rising within him: a call to leave, to take the road to the mountain, on this white road one more time, to become once again shadow, washed, enlarged and then erased by the sun.

He walks alone, dizzy with the scents of summer, on this white road that he cannot see, but that he knows by heart. Vinzel, Luins, Rolle, Yens: he keeps walking east.

At times, when the sun is too harsh, he sits under a tree, removes his cap, wipes his brow. He eats his bread and cheese. He drinks water from his flask.

At nightfall, Julien loses his way. Then, he follows the railroad tracks until the next station. Trains, drowning in white steam, whistle in his ears. He gets to Rolle or Lussy. He climbs on the first train that goes by. Sometimes he gets off in Lausanne, in Neuchâtel, in Pontarlier. He has completely lost track of where he is. He needs a charitable soul to put him back on the right train for him to be able to go home.

One day, he failed to come home.

He was walking in the vineyards with his cane and his little Rollei. It was time for his lunch break. Under an apple tree, some women were seated around cider and dark bread. Laughing joyously, they invited him to join them. Julien sat down in the fresh shade. He drank cider, ate the rye bread and the cheese crumbs. The blazing sun's warmth was crushing. A white haze rose from the vines. The sky over the Jura was entirely cloudless.

Dazed by the scorching heat, Julien fell into a deep sleep.

When he awoke, at the end of the afternoon, the women were gone. There were rumblings of thunder on the mountain tops. The sky was ashen. He set out again, descending towards the lake, and plodded on, conscientiously, until he reached a little country train station where trains don't often stop. He was alone. A dark freezing rain bowed down the yellow wheat. Julien found refuge under the awning, took out a cigarette, cracked a Diamond match.

Three trains came through without stopping.

"No matter what, Julien said to himself, I'm getting on the next one. Even if it is headed for Paris..."

Fortunately, the following train did stop. No one got off. But Julien promptly climbed on board. He found a seat next to a window. Hills, woods, forests: everything seemed to march in front of his eyes as if in an accelerated dream; he became more captivated with each passing second but more dazed as well... Once in a while, he would recognize a church, or at other times a water tower. Mostly he let this torrent of silent images lull him almost to sleep.

The train came to an abrupt stop.

He recognized the match factory, on his left, and the Rue de la Gare, over there, drenched with rain. It was his own good old city of Nyon! He rushed to the door, but then retraced his steps: he had forgotten his camera on the seat.

At that very moment, the train started up again and Julien lost his balance. But he got up again, courageously, ran towards the still open door and, as they so often do in American movies, he leaped out into space.

It is the end of summer.

Red pumps, tanned legs under the light cotton dress, little straw hat: Livia is back.

Very reluctant to see her go, they accompanied her to Porta Susa in the early ghostly morning, Antonio dragging the two heavy suitcases, Nora on Paul's arm and the three young ladies in front, telling each other the latest *barzellette* (jokes).

On the quay, in the midst of the uproar of trains, a sickening mixture of steam and soot, a last hug.

True life is somewhere else, over there, on the other side of the mountain, thinks the secret child. Today is when it begins.

Over there, at the end of the quay, close to the Lyonnaise game of ninepins, a crowd has gathered.

A woman is busy trying to help a man who has fallen on the tracks; he is bleeding profusely, mouth open, hands clutching a camera, eyes staring into empty space.

At the hospital, Julien was in excruciating pain: a broken shoulder blade, both arms smashed to a pulp, bruises on his face, and around his head, an elastic bandage that drives him crazy and keeps him from sleeping.

As the days go by, however, the broken bones mend, the bruises on his face disappear. He can breathe and sleep like before, he can listen to the radio, he can have a drink with his mates.

And then, a miracle occurs!

When the nurse removes the bandage from his eyes, he lets out a cry: the buttered toast, the little jar of orange marmalade and the bowl of coffee, he discovers them in one fell swoop, with only a glance, even before he has had a taste, he has devoured them with his eyes — which, of course, has never happened to him!

And the nurse's smile!

Her heavy blond braids held in place with a little red elastic! The little blue-green halo on her beautiful white coat! The silver and turquoise bracelet on her wrist...

"Pinch me, Mademoiselle!"

The pretty nurse turned around.

"Excuse me?"

He repeated his request.

"Yes, pinch me, bite me, beat me! Do not be afraid!"

She took his hand in hers and gently pinched him.

For the first time, Julien has seen the color of her eyes, a deeply moving bluish mauve, like the lake at dawn, a long time ago, in the oblique rays of the sun when the day is yet to be born.

"My God!"

He buried his face in his hands. He cried out. He looked at the nurse one more time. Then he looked out the window, the gray and green Jura mountains, the sky, clouds running through it, with orange, brown, purple streaks.

"In the name of God! Oh my God, my God!"

As he was thundering, his gaze mesmerized by the beauty of nature, the nurse left the room, only to return a few moments later, a mirror in hand. Julien looked at himself in the mirror for a long time, first in astonishment, and then amused.

"So this is your mug, you old buccaneer!"

He stuck out his tongue, rolled his eyes, examined his teeth. He made a face at himself in the mirror.

"So this is what I look like!"

Suddenly he burst into a fit of laughter, a huge, uncontrollable and contagious laughter.

"Admit it: you were expecting better!"

They meet at the lake.

The air is sweet and transparent. Yvoire appears to be within earshot.

When the boat arrives, it's a scramble! Everyone fights and elbows to occupy the best seats. Pierre and Livia are on the deck, on the first level at the rear of the boat.

They kiss. They brush against each other. And here they are, already on the other side of the lake.

Released from the hospital, he left with no baggage and without a cane.

This old white road: he knows every turn, every tree, every house by heart. But he doesn't recognize it. His pace is unsure. He has trouble breathing. The light is cruel: there is a dizzying cacophony of cries and honking, of thundering vehicles, blinding colors. To protect himself, Julien places his hand in front of his eyes. He blinks. Tears stream down his cheeks. He feels more and more like a foreigner with every step he takes.

Sometimes, when he is alone, Julien shuts his eyes to return to the world he used to know.

It is no use! Light, by erupting into his life, has burned everything. The dark world full of familiar ghosts, where he used to live has disappeared. On certain days, he feels as if his life had only been something he has dreamed.

Originally, these were the Château stables that only left room on each side of the square for a small narrow path. Then they were given to the poor. Finally, the rats and the crows took over.

Today, the location has become a real battlefield with trenches and uprooted trees. The view is now unobstructed all the way to the horizon. You can breathe in the air of the lake. The silhouette of Mont-Blanc looms up behind the towers of the château. Along with the ashes and rubble, steam shovels are clearing away the accursed memories.

Once again, he cannot believe his eyes.

Emilie: her hands moving ceaselessly, as if they suffered from restlessness, her face solemn above a black business suit, organza blouse, cameo at her neck, always neat as a pin!

Julien observes her for hours on end, as he used to do in the courtyard of the school when the old photographer would plant his tripod under the great chestnut tree, when their bodies brushed against each other, when they used to steal away to the local dances and would come home, exhausted, at dawn along paths that might well be unsafe after having danced all night — and now he cannot recognize her.

Now that Livia is back in Switzerland, she has stopped writing to her parents. She does not phone them either. Occasionally a telegram, when Nora's letters are pressing, a few syncopated words to say everything is fine.

More and more often, she manages to slip out of the clinic during the midday break. She runs to the lake, Pierre is waiting for her near the port or under the chestnut trees. They devour a sandwich, hastily, feverishly, kissing each other, oblivious to the sparrows who come begging for a few breadcrumbs.

At two o'clock, Livia runs off. She hurries back to her patients, her syringes and tubes, her small bottles of white pills that she dispenses with generosity. And Pierre returns to his work table, to the telephones that need to be repaired, and to his sullen boss...

Julien who used to be forever out and about, at present locks himself up in the attic. This is where in the middle of the chaos of crates and cardboard boxes, of empty bottles, old LPs, he found all his photos (that he had never seen).

Some are blurry or poorly cropped, others are burned by the light; some are crooked, some curiously focused on unfamiliar characters, on unusual objects on, bizarre scenes — everything he has never been able to see is right here!

Livia, as well, has long been burning with impatience to open the little strong box of images! She has been aware of its presence, ever since her arrival in Switzerland, for it is hidden under a pile of clothes in a corner of the closet in her room, and kept securely under lock and key. She has been strictly forbidden to open it.

One night, however, curiosity gets the best of her: with a screwdriver, she pries open the lock. She finally is able to touch the forbidden images — the images of feast and exile, of glory and disgrace.

The official images, those that were ordered by the Duce, are altered, touched up, cropped, cut, disguised: they represent the gaze of the lion turned on himself, on his subjects, and on the world he holds under total control, or so he believes like a demiurge with absolute power. The hidden images: those of illness, of abandon, of the fundamental powerlessness, of the solitary and lost tyrant: it is the gaze of Antonio, a shifted, ironic, discrete, attentive point of view that reveals the hidden other side of the formal setting, the truth buried beneath the official lies.

A photograph, writes Campo to his daughter Livia, is not a proof that something is real; it does not prove a thing. It does not glorify anything, it does not shed light on anything that is visible. One cannot build a life on images, celebrating them, or trusting them blindly. That is why, whatever their origin, all of the idolatrous religions are doomed to disappear, sooner or later, from the memory of men.

It is the unique print of a glance that drives out ghosts, and elicits the appearance — in moments of grace that are all too rare — a spark of truth in the darkness of the world.

You can never make out his face, but he is there, in the shadows, the secret child, his ghost is lurking in the image. You can almost feel his presence: along the Po, or on the terrace of a country inn, under the great chestnut tree in bloom.

His mouth is open. He wants to scream. He listens. He waits.

Who will deliver him from his secrets?

Every night, Antonio plays the organ at the church of the exiled Vaudois from Piemonte, on Corso Vittorio. He sits in the nave at the helm of his vessel. He is the only commander on board. Under his fingers, cascades of musical notes echo within the walls of the empty church. He leaves port. He pushes the bellows to the maximum. The boat rolls a little. The night is beautiful and studded with stars.

Now he is on high seas!

Eyes closed, Campo navigates only by sight. The sea is dark, rich with luminous islets, chasms, coral reefs. In the shadows, his hand is steady. He cuts an elegant swath through the waves. Every night, he explores more and more deeply the sea within himself, where words are forbidden, where faces and voices melt into silence — this obscure world of a time before images.

Here is the image that holds Julien's eyes. He cannot look away.

Straddling a tricycle, two children are smiling at him: a little boy in short raw linen overalls, bare feet in his sandals, and a little girl in a cotton dress with short sleeves, white socks, short hair with bangs. She is sitting at the back, behind Pierre, her big brother, who is in command of the tricycle. His hands are on the handlebars. He is smiling and beaming: he is protected by his little sister whereas he is the one at the controls.

The two children are glued together as if they were twins. They are both looking towards Julien who cannot see them despite his thick glasses. The little girl has a small silver heart around her neck.

Jacqueline!

Of course, he has not forgotten her face, the fall into the pond, the little white coffin.

Yet, in this image, it is not her. She does not look like the little girl he has loved in the secret place of his memory. She is more lively, independent and naughty.

For all these years, during the dark and deep night in which Julien had plunged head first, he has adored images!

The people he loved — he is astounded to discover — in no way resemble those images.

The same experience, Julien will reiterate it on a daily basis: Pierre has never been that carefree, nonchalant, unmanageable boy, but was, instead, this anxious, silent child who watched over his sister like a guardian angel.

For the first time, thanks to the photos, Julien discovers Emilie's secret: that leg, shorter than the other, which she skillfully hides, either by remaining seated, or by cleverly sliding the left foot under the heel of the right to conceal her limp.

Jacques is different as well: in shorts and hair combed back with brilliantine, he looks mischievous and undaunted. This is not the good child that Julien, deep in his primordial night, had always imagined.

What is it he is hoping to accomplish, the secret child, by exhuming all these photographs? By delving into this world of shadows in search of those anonymous, ignored, silent, heroic figures?

He is looking to restore a name and a face to them. He would like to rediscover their eyes. He wants to repair the silence. He wants to erase the injustice and the omissions of History.

The secret child is the child who is excluded, hidden, abandoned, rejected. He protects a secret that does not exist, for within him everything is secret and everything is blinding light.

In Julien's language, secret (from the Latin *secretus*) speaks of separation, disjunction, cutting off, exclusion, segregation. Since the eighteenth century the "secret" is also the word for a prison, a cell, where a person suspected of plotting against the authorities is thrown into solitary confinement. It is, furthermore, a small personal seal that is applied to private missives.

In German, Antonio's first language, the secret designates the inside of the house *(Geheimnis)*, deep intimacy, concealed shadow, like a hidden danger in the hearth of the family home. In Greek, secret refers to concealment, the code to which the common mortal may not have access: the impenetrable secret that only a few of those rare initiated ones may approach without fear of reprisal.

But a secret is not something, be it an unbearable scene or a haunting image, that needs to be hidden or kept to oneself. If the child is secret, it is, first of all, because he is *other.* He is "*au secret,*" alone like another.

We are all born under the sign of words and images.

It is the name that is given us and that we must inhabit. And it is the image that precedes us, well before we are born that determines what we shall become, observe, believe, love, desire and conceive.

But this word — like a contract that should be honored — is written nowhere and never pronounced. Quite often we spend our life writing it. And this image that sticks to our skin, no one can see it; volatile and truncated like a shadow, it is kept secret until the last second of our last day.

Finally, Livia tells her parents about Pierre. Nora immediately asks:

Is it serious? Does she really love him?

What about him?

His life henceforth is right here.

Pierre has revealed his secret as well.

Her name is Livia. She is a foreigner. For the past two years, she has been working as a nurse at the Métairie.

For the first time, Pierre's eyes met his father's. At first he felt astonishment, then, a searing joy, in the end, melancholy. And what he saw in his father's eyes has become imprinted in his heart like stigmata.

Emilie pinched her lips. She went into the kitchen. In the middle of the rattling and banging of pots and pans, she could be heard repeatedly blowing her nose. When she returned, her eyes were red.

XII

In this photo, I see Nora and Emilie. They are seated in the sun on a low wall by the lake; one is wearing a pretty flowered dress, white hat and white gloves, the other is in black, eyes hidden behind a little veil, as if for a funeral.

Next to them, the men have made an effort to be elegant. Antonio who has given up his mustache, is smiling vaguely in the sunshine, hair slicked back with brilliantine, a copy of *La Stampa* under his arm, cigarette holder between his lips. Behind him, the father of the groom in a brown suit, felt hat on his head, embroidered silk vest and patent leather shoes completing the outfit. His nose is in the stars, his mouth hangs open, and he looks totally surprised: as usual, Julien is looking, elsewhere, off into the distance.

It is the end of summer. A dry wind is blowing in from the lake. The sky is blue and grey.

In the middle of the image, there is a man in black: tall with short hair, a melancholy and handsome face. His name is Pierre. A woman at his side is smiling in her beautiful lace dress. She is radiant. She is no longer a foreigner. Her name is Livia.

Her hands are resting on her round stomach.

Who knows his face?

And who, in the midst of the noisy sounds of summer, can hear his voice?

His name will be Jean. It will be a boy. From each hero of my story, he will borrow a letter, of the alphabet. For example, the first one, the initial, the one from which every story will grow and flourish: Julien, Emilie, Antonio, Nora.

Four cardinal points.

From each one, he will inherit tics, flaws, a penchant for escapades, and strokes of genius: he will be intrepid and silent, a rebel, quarrelsome, impatient, brash, always up for a game, passionate about music and newspapers, a little intuitive, very "voyeur," and something of a hooligan — a foreigner forever at the beginning of his story.

Behind the red curtain, in my domain of blood and water, I auscultate voices. I hallucinate faces, I tear the silence asunder.

My story begins at the moment the image is erased.

www.ingramcontent.com/pod-product-compliance
Lightning Source LLC
Chambersburg PA
CBHW020021030726
47499CB00007B/2216